Young Love in Memphis:

Heart on Reserve

B. Love

Soar young girl. Soar.

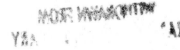

www.authorblove.com
www.blovesbooks.com

Grace

"You think it's gonna be that easy to get rid of me, Grace? Y'all females think y'all can just play with a nigga feelings and let him go when y'all feel like it and we ain't supposed to hurt and feel? Well, I have feelings too, and if you think a woman scorned is nothing to play with, wait until you deal with a nigga who's been hurt and his ego has been bruised. Ima ask you this one time and one time only. Are you sure you want to cut me off… seconds after I tell your trifling ass that I love you?"

This side of Andy wasn't new to me sadly. When I left Memphis to be with him almost two years ago, he was the perfect gentleman. He was sweet, loving, and caring. Andy was gentle and patient with me. Never raised his voice. Never disrespected me. Never laid a hand on me. But then… he slowly began to change.

First, it started with him cheating on me. When we left I was sixteen. A sixteen-year-old virgin. He told me that he would never pressure me for my virginity. That's because we started out as friends… and had a three-year friendship before things turned romantic… the relationship we had went beyond sex. I believed him. Obviously.

We came to California so that he could go to Art school. The plan was for me to finish my last two years of high school and work a part time job while he went to college and worked a part time job as well. He had family here, so they helped me enroll in school and they even helped us get a little one-bedroom apartment.

In the beginning… it was perfect. It was… the most freeing experience of my life. I went from being cooped up in my house with my overbearing and unloving old school strict father and spineless weak mother, to being with the man I'd die for – until his actions started killing me.

He cheated.

The first time he seemed regretful. As if he'd genuinely never do it again. Said he was just stressed out and needed a release. I forgave him and put it behind us. The second time he seemed blameful. As if it was my fault since I wasn't having sex with him. The third time he seemed uncaring. As if my feelings didn't matter.

So, I did what I thought would keep him from cheating. I gave him my virginity. That stopped the cheating alright. But it led to other things. Things that I'd honestly trade in for his cheating. Things like waking me up in the middle of the night after he'd worked and studied and needed sex. Getting mad when I wouldn't give it. Choking me until I lost consciousness and proceeding to take what he wanted without my consent.

Things like inviting all of his newfound rowdy friends to our apartment for sets and parties throughout the week. Expecting me to come home after work and school. Then cook and clean. Then fuck him. Then entertain his guests with him.

Things like taking our money and using it to go on road trips with said friends instead of paying the light and phone bills like he promised he would.

The man I'd die for was an immature ass little boy. And I was a stupid ass little girl for putting up with it. Putting up with it because he was my best friend and safe escape when we were in Memphis. And up until this point, I'd rather deal with his bullshit until I was done with high school than to return home to my parents.

But this last time… I just… couldn't take it anymore. I'd spent my Saturday working double shifts to make sure we'd have the last of our rent. That we were behind four months on. That I knew nothing about. Come home to find not Andy, but three of his bum ass friends chilling on the couch. After sending them away I went into our room and retrieved the bible I'd been hiding money in, figuring Andy's evil behind would never think to open it, and all of the money was gone!

I confronted him about it just a few minutes earlier and he swore he didn't take it. I believed him. I'm sure it was one of his little friends. So I asked him if he could not have them over as much, especially while he was away, and he declined. Said it was his name on the lease and he could have whoever he wanted over.

Ignoring the fact that shortly it wouldn't matter whose name was on the lease because we were both going to be getting kicked out. Sad part about it was he'd have somewhere to go. He could stay with family or move on campus, but as a senior in high school in a completely different state than my parents I had absolutely nowhere else to go.

Finally reaching my breaking point, I told Andy that this was *not* going to work. That I couldn't take living like this anymore. That I'd rather go home and deal with my father than to continue to put up with his foolishness. And he told me he loved me. Told me he loved me as if that would make all of this okay.

I avoided his eyes as tears oozed from mine. The last thing I wanted to do was fight with him. I was tired. So very tired.

"You don't hear me?" Andy taunted while grabbing my forearm.

"How can I not?"

"So what you gon' do, Grace? I know shit has been fucked up lately, but it'll get better baby, I swear. You just have to hang in here with me. I can't do this without you. I'll get the money back. And I won't have anyone else over. Whatever I gotta do to get you to stay I will."

"I'll stay." I gave in in a voice that was so low I hardly heard it myself.

Andy's face flushed over with relief as he pulled me into his arms and hugged me tightly.

"Thank you, Grace. You won't regret this I promise. I'm going to go and get the money right now," he assured me as he released me.

I smiled genuinely. I knew I wouldn't regret it because tomorrow while I was supposed to be at school I was going to be on my way back to Memphis.

Braille

This was not how I planned on spending the start of my spring break. It was the heat of the day. I was on my period. I had a flat tire. And my nephew Reign was in the backseat crying because he was hungry, hot, and just as irritated as I was.

I called my Pops to see if he could come and fix my tire, but he didn't answer his phone. I called my sister Camryn's husband Rule, and he said he was on his way... but that he was thirty minutes away. I'm not the most patient person, so I'd been outside for the past ten minutes trying to change the tire my damn self.

My hair was flat ironed, but I was sweating so much my natural curls were starting to pop out and stick to my head. Eventually I gave up and slid down my car to rest on my tire. Reign's yelling pulled me up from my uncomfortable seat. I opened the backseat door and stuck my head inside.

He stopped crying and smiled at me immediately. This little man was my world. It's crazy because I found out that his mother Camryn was my sister probably a little less than two years ago. Now he's here and I just can't get enough of him. Cam and I are so close it's like we grew up together. And Rule is like the big brother I never had.

Cam and I met in the cutest way. She was having a workshop at her cousin Elle's dance studio and we immediately clung to each other. Probably because we looked so much alike. We both had the same curly hair and gray eyes. Both of which we got from our white Father. To be honest, I've *hated* being mixed most of my life.

I used to wear brown contacts and *beg* my mother to relax my hair. She never did. The most she'd do was let me get a silk press. Now that I'm eighteen and a senior in high school she's given me permission to do whatever I want to my hair. I cut it... but I've grown to love myself and my curls thanks to my big sister. So when I get tired of them I flat iron it, but I don't think I'll ever relax my hair.

Although hot days like this have me tempted.

"What you in here crying about?" My face was serious but Reign never took me seriously.

He grabbed my cheek and pulled me closer to him.

"You need some help?" I heard a voice I didn't know ask behind me.

I slowly turned around and faced the cutest guy I'd seen in a while. We didn't have guys that looked like him in Memphis. He couldn't have been from around the way. If he was... how'd I miss *him* all of my life?

Ole boy's skin was the same light shade as mine, but he had red undertones in his skin. His hair was cut close in a tapered curly afro. With naturally arched eyebrows and tight dark eyes, he looked like a pretty boy... but there was a roughness about him that shined through his eyes. His lips were full and smooth. And he had the cutest beauty mark under his left eye.

I figured he was probably around my age, but his facial hair made him look a little older. Scratching my cheek, I looked him over once more as my phone vibrated in my pocket. The sight of my Pops' name on my screen made me roll my eyes. *Now he wants to call me back.* I pressed ignore and returned my gaze to the cutie in front of me.

"You ain't hear me?" He took a step towards me.

"Huh? Um yea."

"Yea you heard me or yea you need help?"

"Both."

"Aight. Where's your spare?"

I don't know how my face looked but it made him smile.

"My spare?"

"Yea. Your spare tire."

"Um, Ion think I have one of those."

Skepticism covered his face as he walked to my trunk.

"This your car?"

"Yea."

"Pop the trunk."

After I popped the trunk, I went back to the backseat and ran my fingers through Reign's curly hair.

"Your baby daddy ain't shit," I heard the cute stranger say.

"What?" I got out of the car and walked towards him.

"I said your baby daddy ain't shit. How he gone have you out here not knowing how to change your tire or even knowing what a spare tire is?"

"That's not my kid. That's my nephew."

He smiled but lowered his face to hide it as he walked to the front of my car.

"If that was your way of checking my relationship status you could've just asked if I was single."

"Whatever. Take him out the backseat so I can hike the car up."

"Fine."

I grabbed Reign from his car seat and carried him to the nearest tree so we'd be under the shade.

"Can you believe him, Reign? All in my business like he knows me."

Reign nodded as if he understood every word I said. I smiled and continued to play with him until I saw Rule's car pull over to the side of the road. Standing, I put Reign on one side of my hip and wiped my pants just in case I had any dirt or rocks on me.

"Sorry 'bout that, lil sis. I got here as fast as I could," Rule spoke walking towards us.

"It's cool. He's taking care of it."

I pointed towards the cutie whose name I didn't even know.

"Zo?" Rule called.

He stood and looked over at us with a smile.

"What's up, Rule? I ain't seen or heard about you since you and Power got out the game."

"Hell yea. We legit now. What about you, young nigga?"

Zo shrugged and looked at him. "This your blood sister?"

Rule smiled and took Reign from my arms.

"Nah. She's my wife's sister, but as long as you're in the streets she's off limits to you."

"How y'all gon' talk about me like I'm not right here?"

Rule kissed my temple and walked over to my car.

"You want me to take Reign home? Or you still got some shit planned for y'all to do?"

"Nah. You can take him. I was about to go up to The University of Memphis to see about scheduling a campus tour, then I was going to take him home. I think he's hungry, though. He was kind of cranky."

"You thinking about going there?" Zo asked as he returned to my tire.

"Yea this fall." I kissed Reign's cheek then grabbed his bag from my backseat. "Tell Cam I'll call her when I get home later tonight. Thanks for coming," I said to Rule as I handed him Reign's bag.

"Aight. You need to come over this weekend so I can show you how to change your tire. It's a good thing Zo showed up, but what if you wouldn't have been able to get in touch with me? Did you call Edward?"

"He didn't answer his phone. I don't even know why he has a cell phone. He never answers it. He called me back but Zo was here so I didn't answer."

Rule smiled and shook his head. "Call that man back, B."

"I'll call when I get home."

"Aight. I'll see you later."

"Bye. Bye, baby!"

Reign looked back at me and smiled. He was the most handsome baby in life. With our gray eyes and his Father's dimples and freckled cheeks he was going to be a heartbreaker when he grew up.

Zo pulled my attention away from Reign by asking, "You got a boyfriend?"

"Are you a drug dealer?"

"What kind of question is that?"

"What kind of answer is that?"

"What's your name?"

"Braille. What's your name?"

"Zo."

"Your full name."

"Lorenzo, but as you can see everyone calls me Zo."

"Are you a drug dealer, Lorenzo?"

He smiled and I frowned to keep from doing so.

"I see you like to go against the grain, Braille."

"Thank you for changing my tire."

"How old are you?"

"Eighteen. You?"

"Same. Senior?"

"Yea."

"Do you have a boyfriend?"

"I don't want one. Especially a drug dealing one."

"I ain't no drug dealer."

"Then what are you?"

"A nigga that provides for me and mine by any means."

Why was that so sexy? I stepped back to put some space between us. He stepped forward and grabbed my shirt – pulling me closer to him.

"Why you running away?"

"It's hot out here and I'm already sweating my hair out. I need to go."

"I'm hungry. Thank me by grabbing a bite to eat with me."

"Nu unh. I thanked you by thanking you. Besides, you heard what Rule said."

Zo nodded and released my shirt. "Give me your number then."

"No. Thanks. Now put that flat tire in my trunk so I can go."

He looked at me sideways like he wanted to say some slick shit, but he nodded and did as I said instead.

Zo closed my trunk and leaned against it. "Follow me down the street. We can head to Midtown and grab something to eat."

"Didn't you hear what I just said?"

"Yea, I heard you. Did you hear me?"

"I heard you."

"Now that we've gotten that out the way get in your car and follow me like I said."

"Lorenzo, I don't know who…"

The closeness of his body to mine shut my mouth instantly. He leaned down as if he was about to kiss me, but he just… stared into my eyes instead.

"Why you giving me such a hard time, Braille? I'm not asking you to marry me. All I'm asking is that you eat with me. I changed your tire under this hot ass sun. You mean to tell me you can't sit with a nigga for thirty minutes and just chill?"

As I released a hard breath I pushed him away from me gently.

"Fine," I mumbled heading to get in my car.

Zo grabbed me from behind and kept me from opening the door. After he opened it for me, Zo looked me over once more then returned to his car. I got inside of mine, inhaled a deep breath, and gave myself a pep talk the entire drive to wherever it was he decided to take me.

Jessica

"You know, I always thought I'd be the one who took you to your prom."

Those words. That voice. I hadn't seen Cameron in months, but there was no mistaking his voice. I couldn't even turn around. Tears immediately filled my eyes. I dropped the box that I was grabbing from the backseat of the car absently and inhaled a deep breath.

Cameron Green.

My first love. My first *real* lover.

I met Cameron through two ladies that I adopted as my older sisters – Alayziah and Layyah. A while back I was raped by Chris – my deceased sister Jasmine's baby daddy. I already hated him because I felt like he was the reason Jasmine died. Their relationship was so toxic. She was so lovesick over him that she started drinking and doing all kinds of drugs. Eventually she overdosed and left her daughter to be raised by my mother.

Chris came around every once in a while, but not enough to give him credit for it. One day when he came over… he decided to take what didn't belong to him. My virginity. After that, not only did I not want to have anything to do with love, but I didn't want to have anything to do with men period.

Cameron changed all of that.

It took him hardly any time at all to break down my walls and fill the holes along my heart and soul with his love. Because he's a year older than me, he left for college the start of my senior year of high school. He chose to go to Morehouse. Instead of allowing space and distance to pull us apart, I decided that it would be best if we ended our relationship when he left about seven months ago.

I'd seen him a few times since then but not for long. Eventually it got to the point where when he visited he didn't even let me know. Then we stopped calling each other as much. That led to fewer and fewer text messages.

So, for him to be standing behind me… I couldn't believe it.

"What are you doing here?" I asked with my back still to him.

"I just wanted to see you. Layyah told me that you were getting your prom dress this weekend. I was… wondering if… I could take you."

I turned around and faced the young man I'd prepared to live the rest of my life without. His shoulder length curly hair blew in the wind. I ran my fingers along the curve of his strong jaw. Cameron was a masterpiece.

He removed one of his hands from his pocket and pulled me into him. Chest to chest, I looked up and into his eyes.

"I miss you," he mumbled before kissing my forehead.

"I miss you too. How's school going?"

"I didn't come here to talk about all of that. Yes, or no?"

Taking a step back, I ran my fingers along the tattoo on my wrist. The first night I gave myself to him sexually we decided to get matching tattoos. We ended up getting *Wild is the Wind* on our wrists. Nina Simone's rendition of that song was playing while we waited to get tatted and we both agreed that that song fit us perfectly.

"Cameron, how do you think we're going to get over each other if you take me to my prom?"

"I never planned on getting over you, Jessie. You broke up with me, but I never broke up with you."

"You stopped calling and texting. You didn't even tell me you were home these last couple of times. I had to find out from Lay and on Facebook."

"I got tired of you rejecting me. You know how much that shit hurts? To love somebody so fucking much and they just consistently step on your heart and say to hell with your feelings?"

"Cameron… you know that's not the case. I just… thought it would be easier for us if we split."

"Easier for who, Jessica? Because this is killing me."

Truth of the matter was; I'd seen what could happen when love wasn't returned correctly. After my sister practically killed herself, I vowed to never let love overtake me. No matter how much I loved Cameron… I just couldn't see myself ever fully committing to him or anyone else.

"I'm sorry. I never meant to hurt you. I guess in my attempt to keep from getting hurt I hurt you. I'm sorry."

He nodded and sighed heavily.

"You already have a date for your prom or what?"

"No. I was going to go alone or with a couple of girlfriends."

"May I take you?"

"You came all the way back to Memphis to ask me if you could take me to my prom?"

"Yes, and for this…"

His fingers went into the strands of my hair and he pulled me into him. My hands automatically cupped his cheeks as he took my lips into his.

I melted into his body and shivered when his arms wrapped around me. The feel of his tongue wrapping around mine had me moaning and running my hands down his chest. God, I missed him. He pulled himself away from me and I laid my head on his chest.

"Yes," I almost whispered.

"What colors do I need to wear?"

"Well, my dress is a two-piece cream set with red and yellow flowers at the bottom."

"Let me see it."

I removed myself from his body unwillingly and picked up the box I dropped at the sound of his voice. When I opened it he took a couple of pictures and I closed it back up.

"How long will you be in town?"

"Just right now. I only came for you."

A smile covered my face as I pulled my hair behind my ear.

"Well don't I feel special."

"You are special. You ain't figured that out yet?"

Cameron's fingers intertwined with mine and I made my way back inside of his chest.

"You have class in the morning?"

"Sadly."

My breath came out hard as I pulled myself away from him.

"You should probably go then so you won't be all night getting back."

He nodded in agreement but remained in front of me. I smiled and tilted my head.

"I love you, Jessie."

"I love you too. Call me and let me know you made it back safely."

"Do you?"

"I do."

"I need you to start acting like it."

I nodded but remained silent. He kissed my forehead again and I watched him go back to his car. When he drove off, I went inside of my brother Jabari's home and put my dress in the closet of the room I slept in. I was at his house more than I was at my own. He had a nice little set up for me.

I took a shower, ate, then plopped down in the middle of my bed. Resisting the urge to call Cameron, I tried calling my old best friend Grace yet again. Ever since she moved to California we hardly talked anymore. She didn't answer the phone, like I thought she wouldn't, so I took a nap.

When I woke up it was close to ten p.m. Cameron should have been back on campus by eight, so I texted him.

Me: Why didn't you call me and let me know you made it back?

Love You: *Never made it.*

Me: Where are you?

Love You: *In the room we made love in… thinking about you.*

Me: Cameron.

Me: I'm on my way.

Hanif

"You better believe by the time you done with that bitch and you hit my line I'll have a new lineup!" My go to Olivia yelled as I left the room I'd rented for us the night before.

She'd never been to my crib and I planned on keeping it that way. Not because I had a girlfriend who liked to randomly pop up, even though I did, but because I didn't trust Olivia. Really, I didn't trust nobody. Not even my girl Pria.

That's why I fucked around. Kept myself from getting attached to her, catching feelings, and then getting hurt because she betrayed me. She swore she wouldn't, but her word didn't mean shit to me.

I was about to hop in my ride when I saw a chick struggling with her grocery bags. She had about ten in each hand. Like she was determined to not have to take another trip to her car. I started to help her, but she looked so young I didn't want her Pops or somebody questioning me so I continued to my car.

I can't lie, I turned around to cop another look. She was a cute little thing. Her skin was the color of cinnamon and it glowed naturally under the sun. She had long ass straight hair. Looked like it stopped in the middle of her back. I was tempted to run my fingers through it to see if it was real, so I put my hands in my pockets to keep from walking over and trying to do so.

She had the prettiest dark brown slanted eyes. Made her look like... no one I'd ever seen before. Her nose was small and her eyebrows were thin, arched, and real. Not drawn on looking thick as hell like Olivia's. Swear I'll never understand why females cut all their eyebrows off just to draw them junts back on.

She was petite, but she had nice sized breasts. Like they would fit perfectly in my hands. But she looked so damn young. I turned around when I caught a glimpse of her small round ass to keep from lusting after her, but when I did I heard glass shattering and cans hitting the ground.

Most of her bags had slipped from her hands and her groceries were rolling around on the ground. After dropping the rest of her bags she fell to her knees and started crying hysterically. I looked around and groaned. If nobody else went to go and see about her crybaby ass I was gon' be forced to.

When nobody stepped up I ran my hand down my neck and slowly walked over to her. Wrapping my hands around her forearms, I lifted her to her feet. She looked into my eyes then started crying even harder. I pulled her into my chest and stroked her back lightly.

I was hoping that would shut her up but she just kept crying.

"Why you out here crying? Just pick this shit up," I mumbled into her hair.

I couldn't resist running my nose over it to smell it and see if I felt any tracks. None. Her hair was real.

"It's not that simple." Her voice was soft, low, and light.

Pulling her out of my chest I wiped her tears away. She was talking about something bigger than this food on the ground, but I was trying to determine if I cared enough to ask why.

"Why you out here crying?" I repeated.

"Because it's hot."

I looked at her skeptically as I released her.

"You crying because it's hot outside?"

"Yea."

"Your car don't have any air?"

Looking behind her I took in the beat up Hyundai Accent she was driving. It was dirty and old. Probably *didn't* have any air.

"No. It's... so much wrong with it. I drove it from San Francisco. It's practically falling apart. I'm just hot and irritated and tired. I'm sorry."

She wiped fresh tears and turned away from me to start picking up her groceries.

"You drove all the way to Memphis from Cali in this car? What year is it?"

"Ninety-seven."

"How long that take you?"

She shrugged. "What day is it?"

"Friday."

"A week."

There were so many questions floating around in my mind. But instead of asking any of them I helped her pick up her groceries.

"Why the hell you try to take all these bags at one time?" I asked her when we started heading for what I assumed to be her room.

"I told you it's hot. I didn't want to have to make a second trip."

If she didn't look so pitiful I would've laughed at her.

"So you were about to have a mental breakdown trying to carry all this shit at one time instead of just making two trips?"

She nodded and opened the door to her room.

"How old are you?"

"I'm seventeen."

"Where your parents at?" She shrugged and looked away from me. "Who you staying here with?"

"Nobody."

Once I put her groceries on the counter I scratched my head and looked around the room.

"Give me your keys," I ordered softly.

She obviously had a lot going on right now and could use some help. I still wasn't completely sure if I wanted to know what was going on with her, but I'd feel like less of a man if I didn't at least make sure she was half straight before I left.

"Give you my keys?"

"Yea."

In her childlike innocence she gave me her keys without asking any questions. To show her that she could trust me I gave her my phone... locked of course.

"I'm about to take your car to the shop and get your air and whatever else is wrong fixed."

"No... you don't... have to..."

Her eyes started watering so I turned to leave. I couldn't take seeing her cry again.

"Listen, I'm not... I can't pay you back. I mean I can... but I'm saving my money."

"Did I ask you to pay me back?" I turned around to face her. Lowering her head, she shook it no. "What's your name?"

"Grace."

"Will you be okay here by yourself for a couple of hours, Grace?"

Returning her eyes to mine she nodded. I nodded and continued to walk out of the room. As it closed I heard her mumble, "Thanks."

Grace

I can't imagine how crazy I looked sobbing in the middle of this hotel parking lot. To be honest... I didn't even care. I needed that cry. I can't think of the last time I really just cried over the mess I'd gotten myself in following behind Andy almost two years ago.

Drained of my energy, when those bags busted, it was like... my eyes and my heart did as well. Then *he* came up and grabbed me and just made me feel ten times worse. I don't even know his name, but my God was he handsome.

Milk chocolate skin, full brown lips, thick eyebrows, hypnotic brown eyes, long curly eyelashes, and a pierced nose made him look like a god. There were a few tattoos covering his arms, and his head was shaved. He looked good as hell. That made me cry even harder. This fine man was standing in front of me and I'm outside crying like a baby.

My heart was just so heavy. I ended up having to sell my Camaro to get a few thousand for my trip home. And I took the money we were supposed to use to pay the rent. Andy had been blowing my phone up so much I called and got my number changed on the way to Memphis.

When I left Memphis to go with Andy I didn't tell my parents. I wrote them a note and had my friend Elle and her husband who used to be my Coach, Power, give it to them. You'd think if their sixteen-year-old daughter went thousands of miles away from home they'd come get her or call her. My parents did neither. So, instead of going home I used my fake ID to rent me a hotel room for the week.

With my eighteenth birthday one month away, I figured if I could just make it through the summer without them finding out I was back home I'd be straight. I'd find a way to reenroll in school here, graduate, and head right back out of Memphis for college.

The first thing I did after putting up the groceries we were able to salvage was take me a nice long shower. I tried to watch TV and wait for whatever his name was to return but I was tired and he was taking entirely too long, so I laid down and prepared to take a nap. But as soon as I began to dose off he was knocking.

I sat on the edge of the bed and inhaled and exhaled a few deep breaths before standing and slowly making my way to the door. That's when it hit me… I didn't know anything about this man besides he was nice but mean at the same time. He could have come in here and tried to do God only knows what to me. But after what I'd just gone through with Andy… I really didn't even care.

I opened the door wide enough for him to enter with two to-go boxes of food in his hands. He didn't acknowledge me. Just walked through the kitchenette area and sat on the edge of the bed. When he sat one of the boxes on the side of him he looked at me until I started walking back to the bed.

"You eat hot wings?" He asked handing me the box.

"Yea, thanks. How much was it?"

Ignoring me, he grabbed the remote and changed the channel.

"You're mean," I mumbled putting the food back down.

Ignoring me yet again, he stood and washed his hands.

"You not gon' wash your hands, Grace?"

"I'm not hungry."

"What have you eaten today?"

"I drank some water on the road."

"Man, get up and wash your hands so you can eat."

I rolled my eyes, crossed my arms over my chest, and shook my head.

"If I wanted to be told what to do I would've went back home."

"Why didn't you? Your parents dead or some shit?"

"No, my parents are not dead. They're just… not good parents."

"Will you please wash your hands and eat so I can leave with peace of mind?"

Even though I honestly had no appetite, I did as he asked and began to gradually force the fries and wings into my stomach. By the time he was done I'd eaten about three wings. He sighed and pulled a set of keys from his pocket that didn't belong to me.

"Your car is going to be in the shop for about a week. You can use that one until I get it out. You got some money?"

My eyes watered and I lowered my head.

"I told you I did, but I don't want to spend it getting that car fixed."

"I mean for your pockets. Don't worry about getting the car fixed. I'm taking care of that."

Our eyes met, briefly, then he looked away.

"Why?"

"Consider it my good deed for the year."

"I'll pay you back. Just let me get back in school and find another job and I'll pay you back."

"Don't worry about that. If you want to pay me back just… get in school and move in with somebody. You're too young and pretty to be staying in this hotel room by yourself."

My smile was soft as I twirled a piece of hair around my fingers.

"You think I'm pretty?"

"You don't?"

I blushed, causing him to look away.

My mouth opened and closed before I asked, "What's your name?"

"Why?"

"How can you ask me all of these questions and do all of this for me and not even tell me your name?"

"Hanif."

"Hanif, someone has been blowing your phone up with calls and text messages."

"Probably Pria. Where my phone at?"

I stood and went to get his phone off of the desk.

"Who is Pria?"

"My girl."

My grip on his phone tightened. *His girl? The hell was he being all nice to me for if he had a girlfriend?*

"Oh, well… thanks again."

He didn't take my dismissal of him seriously because he kicked his shoes off and handed me his box.

"Toss that for me, Grace."

I took the box from his hands and he went up the bed and rested his back against the headboard.

"I ain't having sex with you," I informed him quickly.

"Chill out. I don't want you to."

"Then why are you getting comfortable?"

"Ima chill here for a minute."

After handing him his phone I went to the other side of the bed and sat down so close to the edge that half of my body was hanging off. He grabbed my right arm and pulled me to the middle of the bed.

"Relax. Ain't nobody gon' hurt your young ass."

"How old are you?"

"Twenty-six."

"What were you doing here?" Hanif licked his lips and returned his attention to the TV. "You have a bad habit of ignoring people."

"I was kicking it with a friend."

"A friend?"

"Yea. A friend."

"A woman?" He nodded. "So you're a cheater?"

"And you're a runaway."

"I'm not a runaway."

"Then what are you, Grace?" This time I ignored him. "Ima head out."

"Wait… I…"

He looked back at me as he grabbed his shoes.

"You what? Look, I don't feel comfortable leaving you here alone. But I ain't for all this conversation. There's nowhere else you can go?"

I could have called Elle, but I wouldn't feel comfortable crashing her place now that she and Coach Power were married with a new baby boy. I could have called Braille or Jessica, but I didn't want their parents trying to get in touch with mine. Had I gone over to any of my family member's houses they would've called my parents too. So really, there was no place else for me to go.

"No. I ain't got nowhere else to go."

"Pack your shit up."

"For what?"

"You're going to follow me to my spot."

"No. That's… I can stay here. I'll be fine."

"I'll sleep better if I know you're okay, Grace."

"Why do you care?"

"I'm still trying to figure that out myself."

I nodded and stood. For some reason I felt safe with him. Then Andy's change came to me.

"I think I should just stay here, Hanif. But thanks. I'm going to be fine."

He let out a deep sigh and put his shoes back down.

"I guess I'm staying here for the night," he mumbled pulling his phone and keys out of his pockets.

"You really don't have to…"

"Listen, I don't want to be here as much as you don't want me to be here so you can come to my place and stay in my guest room or I'll just have to stay here. Either way it goes I can't just leave you. Leave you alone. Here. By yourself.

The whole time he talked his words were going in one ear and out of the other. All I could do was stare into his mouth at his crowded teeth on the bottom. I could see that he was human. He was flawed. He wasn't a perfect guardian angel that found me at my lowest and would leave me to never appear again.

"Grace…"

"Stay."

Hanif nodded and took a step back.

"In the morning we're coming up with a plan for you because this shit…." He held his arms up and pointed around the room. "Ain't gon' work."

"Okay."

"I'm about to take a shower. And I don't like to talk about myself. So chill with the questions when I come out."

"Whatever."

His mouth opened and his eye twitched, but he didn't say anything. He just walked away.

Braille

I sat at the booth I'd chosen for Grace and I and watched her interact with a man I'd never seen before. And when I say man... I mean MAN! This was no high school boy. He was fine as hell. Actually, he looked kind of like Tupac. Bald head and all.

Man, I missed Grace so much. We met our eight grade year at Kirby Middle. Then we started at Kirby High together before she left our tenth grade year following behind Andy's no good ass. There was always something about him that didn't sit well with me.

I tried to talk her out of it but she didn't listen. She said she knew him and trusted him. Said he'd been there for her for years and helped her deal with her crazy parents so she owed her loyalty to him. I'm guessing since she's back in Memphis that didn't work out the way she thought it would.

Saying I'm surprised that she's back would be an understatement. And I'm even more surprised that she called me and asked to meet up with me. Yea, we used to be best friends and super close, but when she left... that changed. Before this morning I hadn't talked to her on the phone in months, but we texted every once in a while. Mostly just a *Hey, I miss you, bye* kind of thing.

Watching Grace with her dude immediately took me back to my time with Lorenzo. He's... weird. He's a senior at Melrose High. He went from being a straight A basketball playing student with multiple scholarships lined up to a drug dealing street kid with no plans of going to college all in one year. Right after his father died of lung cancer. I guess Lorenzo called himself taking his Father's place as their provider.

He stopped playing basketball and spent most of his days with his sisters and mother and nights in the streets. Said he had to be the man of the house and help with the bills. I'm sure his mother appreciated the help, but what kind of mother would strip their child's future away like that?

That just didn't sit well with me. I felt like there was more to the story than he was telling me. I could understand him holding back because that was our first day of knowing each other, but I planned on getting more details about that. And soon.

I know Rule told me that I was off limits for Lorenzo if he was in the streets, but there's something about him that I'm drawn to. Like a magnet. There's something inside of him that pulls me to him. So, if I have to keep my relationship with him a secret I will. *What relationship?* We're not in a relationship. We've only kicked it once.

Let me slow my ass down.

Camryn bought me a car for my eighteenth birthday last month and with it seeing Zo would be no problem. We would just have to make sure wherever we went we chose places I wouldn't run the risk of seeing anyone I knew.

Grace wrapped her arms around her dude and he looked awkward and hesitant. Like he wasn't sure if he should hug her back or not. When he did finally hug her back a look of relief covered his face and he squeezed her and ran his nose over the top of her head. She looked up at him and smiled but it faded quickly.

He must have said something she didn't want to hear because she mugged him and walked away from him and into the restaurant. I chuckled as he said something to her angrily but she ignored him while she opened the door to the café.

Ole dude waited until she walked over to my table before he shook his head and walked away.

"B!" She yelled as I stood.

We embraced and I held her as tight and long as I could.

"Grace, baby, where the hell you been?"

She sighed and we sat down at the same time.

"San Fran."

"Well first, who was that and why was he mad?"

"That's Hanif. He's just naturally mean. He told me he was about to check on my car and see if they had an estimate for it yet, but when he picked me up we were going to go and talk to my folks depending on how my lunch with you went."

"What happened to your car?"

"Girl, I don't know. Life happened to that car. I drove it here from Cali so it's going through it right now. He took it to the shop for me yesterday and they told him it'll be about a week before they could get to it, but his impatient ass thinks if he goes up there harassing them that will make them go faster. He gave me his second car to drive, but he didn't believe I would actually meet with you like I said I would so he wanted to bring me."

She rolled her eyes and I chuckled.

26

"I ordered for us already if you don't mind. I remembered what you like to eat."

"Yea, that's cool."

"So how long you been knowing this nigga?"

"Since yesterday."

"And he getting your car fixed and shit already?"

Grace shrugged and took a sip of the lemonade I ordered for her.

"You having sex with him?"

"Nah. He don't want me like that."

"What makes you say that?"

"He has a girlfriend. Besides, he's old and keeps reminding me that I'm young."

I started to tell her about how he looked when he hugged her. That wasn't the expression of a man who didn't want her. But I decided to let it go and allow her to figure it out in her own time. She pulled her wallet from her purse and pulled a twenty out.

"How much was my food?" She asked sliding me the twenty.

"Girl, put that back. I'm just happy you called. I missed you so much."

"I missed you too."

"What the hell happened?"

Grace ran her fingers through her hair and sighed heavily.

"B, that shit went left out of nowhere. You know I was supposed to go to school and work part time, right?"

"Right."

"I ended up having to work fulltime. So when I was saying I was busy I was real live busy. As soon as I left school I went to the restaurant. I ate there. Worked until we closed. Got home. Showered. Did my homework. Then had to deal with Andy and his friends Most of the time I worked doubles on Saturdays. The only time I really had to rest was Sunday nights and I spent those sleeping when I could."

"Damn. Was Andy not working or some shit?"

"He was, but he was being reckless with the money. When I left we were months behind on the rent because he was taking the money and spending it going on trips and shit with his bum ass friends. Swear I can't stand none of their asses. You know the cost of living is higher there than here, so I got paid way more money there. That's how I was able to send you that money to buy me that Camaro here and have it shipped to me. But I had to sell that just to be able to make sure I had some money to get here and maintain myself until I got another job."

"Awww I loved your car! That Camaro was beautiful!"

"I know. I loved it too, but I had to do what I had to do. I'm just glad to be away from Andy."

"So what did your parents say?"

"Nothing. They don't know I'm here."

"Does Elle know? I started to tell Cam that I was meeting you for lunch."

Elle was my cousin through Cam. We had the same daddy but different mamas. Grace and Elle knew each other before Cam and I knew each other. Grace went to a couple of workshops that Elle had at Kirby and at Elle's dance studio. Elle ended up marrying Power, who was Grace's P.E and African American history teacher. And Cam married Power's younger brother Rule.

"Nah. I haven't told her or Coach Power yet."

"Then where are you staying?"

"Extended Stay."

"In a hotel??" She nodded and took another sip of her lemonade. "Is that where you met Hanif?"

"Yep. He was leaving from visiting some chick. I dropped all of my bags and he helped me. I started crying and he... helped me."

Our number was called so we got up and got our food. I saw her slide the twenty-dollar bill in my purse as I grabbed some extra napkins and I shook my head. Grace was one of the most independent people I knew. Especially at such a young age. I guess she felt like she had to be because her parents were so disconnected from her life. Which is why I was super surprised to hear her say she was letting Hanif help her.

"So what's up, Grace? You get all low eyed and sad looking when you need something and you've been looking like that since you walked in."

"Well... Hanif doesn't want me staying at the hotel by myself..."

"Neither do I."

"He asked me to move in with him, but after watching Andy switch up on me so quick I'm not trying to go there again. So, he told me that I had to find somewhere else to stay or he was going to be at my hotel room with me every night."

"As fine as he is I wouldn't mind."

"Braille!"

"What? I'm just saying. Ole boy is fine."

"Ain't he though?" She blushed and looked into the distance.

I smiled and shook my head.

"So, what? You wanna stay with me and my mama?"

"Just until school is over. Then I'll leave. I can give her some money upfront and pay her monthly."

"Now you know she not gon' take that money, but I'm sure she won't mind you staying with us. She asks about you on a weekly basis. You know you were like a second daughter to her."

Grace nodded as her eyes glossed from tears.

"Yea, well, I appreciate this."

"It's cool. I'd rather have you with me than Andy any day. I never liked him."

"I know. I should've listened."

"Have you registered for school yet?"

"Not yet. I'm going to talk to Coach Power and see if he can help me get back in without my parents having to be involved. I don't want them to know I'm here."

"When are you going to go and talk to him?"

"After I leave here. Ima get Hanif to take me to get my stuff and load the car up then make my way over there. That should give you enough time to ask your mama for me."

"Aight that'll work. She's going to say yes, though. I'll text you. When did you get your number changed? I didn't know who you were this morning."

"On my way back. Andy was blowing my shit up. You know I have no patience for that kind of stuff. When I'm over a person or situation I cuts it or them off completely."

"I already know."

I sat back in my seat and we looked at each other briefly before sharing a smile.

"I missed you, B."

"I missed you too, Grace. Welcome home."

Jessica

I hated saying goodbye to Cameron. One would think with the passing of time it would get easier, but it actually got harder. When I met him last night it was at the same hotel we shared together last summer.

After I told him about having my virginity taken from me by Chris, I told him that I wanted to choose the next man I gave myself to. And I chose him. I don't regret my choice at all. He was so loving. So gentle. So patient. He took his time with me and made sure I was comfortable and enjoying the experience.

If I wasn't so scared of loving and losing myself, Cameron would be perfect for me. He headed out for Atlanta this morning and I missed him already. Instead of going home and spending the day there, I went to one of my family's restaurants. We have two. One in Midtown and one in East Memphis. My brother is the head chef at the one in Midtown. My mom is the head chef at the East Memphis location. She signed the business license for the East Memphis location over to me.

So it's like it belongs to me, but it's really still hers. I get ten percent of our monthly earnings, and when she retires I'm supposed to take over completely, but that's never been the life I wanted. Cooking has been her and my brother Jabari's passion for as long as I could remember. I love waitressing and interacting with people and collecting tips, but as far as running the place and cooking is concerned… that's just not for me.

My passions are entertainment and helping people. This fall when I start college I'm going to major in Mass Communications with an emphasis in Journalism. I'm going to be the next Oprah. A new, young, and fresh Oprah.

Halfway into my impromptu shift I received a call from my homegirl Grace. She told me that she was back in town and wanted to link up later tonight. I happily agreed because I hadn't seen her in almost two years. I've never been the type to have female friends, but I kicked it with her and Braille while in school. My tenth grade year we went out a couple of times, but after the shit that happened with Chris went down, I kind of shut everybody out except for my brother RiRi, Alayziah, and their friends.

Grace and I decided to link up with Braille and go out to eat and bowling or something tonight, so I was prepared to end my shift a little early to go home and get ready. Braille and I agreed that if we both went to The University of Memphis we'd live on campus together. Now that Grace was back... hopefully she could join us and the three musketeers would be back together again.

After turning my apron in and clocking out I got in RiRi's old car that I'd practically taken as my own and headed home. When I made it I pulled my phone out of my purse to check the time and saw that I had a missed call from Cameron. I happily sat in my beanbag and called him back.

"Jessie..."

"Hey, baby. What's up?"

"I was just calling to let you know I made it back to campus."

"Good. I miss you already."

He was silent for a few seconds and that made me smile even harder. Most guys tried to act hard, but Cameron never hid his feelings from me.

"I miss you too, Jessica. I enjoyed you last night."

My bottom set of lips throbbed just at the thought.

"I enjoyed you too. Very much."

"You know I didn't come home just to sex you up, right?"

"I know."

"I just wanna make sure. Not that I'm complaining."

"I'd rather you get it from me than someone else."

"I don't want it from anyone else. I don't want nobody else period. All I want is you."

"So when can I see you again?"

"Whenever you want to, Jessie."

"Okay. Well. Whenever you're free..."

"Just give me a date."

"I don't want to. I don't know your schedule."

"Just give me a date."

"Next Saturday."

"Done."

"Just like that?"

"Just like that."

"Cameron…"

"I told you before I even left for school that I would do whatever it took to make this shit work. I don't know why you won't take me for my word."

"I do… it's just…"

My eyes watered at the thought of my sister. How she loved so hard and gave so much and died with so little.

"You're not your sister, Jessica. And I ain't that nigga that did her wrong and did that shit to you. I'm tired of being punished for that."

"You're right. I'm sorry."

"I don't want you to be sorry. I just want you to stop."

"Okay," I mumbled as tears slid down my cheeks.

"Okay? Okay what?"

"I'll stop."

"Okay."

"Cam?"

"Yes, baby?"

"Will you be my boyfriend again?"

He grew silent again and I smiled.

"I've always been your boyfriend, girl. I told you I never broke up with you."

"Fine. Well, I need to get ready to head out and meet B and Grace."

"Okay. Call me when you get home and settled. Facetime me."

"K, I love you."

"I love you too."

I disconnected the call and allowed my phone to fall from my hand onto the carpeted floor. I didn't know how this long distance shit was going to play out. I didn't know how long it would last. If he would remain as loyal, faithful, and genuine as he's always been. All I knew was that I loved him. And he swore he loved me too. And at this point in my life, that's all I needed.

Cameron

I was surprised as hell when Jessie asked me to be her man again. She was so closed off and guarded I figured we'd never commit to each other again. I loved her with all that was within me, but I was slowly pulling myself from her. Not because I didn't want her anymore, but because I was tired of waiting for her to want me enough to commit to me.

Since she *did* commit to me again I had to get up with my girl Markeda and let her know shit was about to change. Markeda and I met when I was in high school. Our friendship had always been strange. We were friends, but we fucked around every once in a while. My family didn't want me to be with her because they thought she was a bad influence on me when we were younger, and honestly I think that made me want to be in a relationship with her more than anything.

When I committed to Jessie last summer me and Markeda stopped kicking it as much. Then, Jessica broke up with me and I left for school. Markeda attends Spelman so... our friendship just... came back alive.

We kick it almost every other day when we're free and I throw her the dick once a week. But she understood that that was only because I couldn't have Jessie. Now that I had her back we were going to have to go back to a normal friendship.

If I knew Markeda as well as I thought I did she... wasn't going to make this shit easy. She was scheduled to work today at the library on campus, so I figured if I told her there she'd be on chill and not give me such a hard time. I slid in there and ignored the stares from all the chicks in there and found my way to her.

She looked up at me and smiled.

"What are you doing here?" Markeda whispered standing.

"I need to talk to you."

"About what?"

"Jessica and I are back together now."

She shrugged and looked around as if that had nothing to do with her.

"Okay, and?"

"And I can't fuck with you like that no more. We can still be cool but no more sex. And we can't be spending all that time together no more."

"I swear I'm so tired of you and that girl. One minute you with her and the next you in my bed. Y'all need to get it together."

"We got it together now."

Markeda exhaled loudly and rolled her eyes. She shook her head and sat back down.

"Whatever, Cammy. You'll be back next week."

"No I'm not. We're done. I love you like my sister but that's it."

"So you fuck your sister? Get outta here with that shit." I chuckled and started walking away. "Cam, wait."

I stopped and gave her time to make her way to me.

"You know I love you. Not as my damn brother either. I already have two of those. I don't need no more."

"Well, I said we can still be cool. Just no more sex."

"Fine," she mumbled before walking away.

I hated putting her in her feelings like this, but what can I say? As long as she made herself available to me I was gon' take full advantage of it.

Grace

When I woke up this morning and felt Hanif's arm wrapped around me I realized I'd just awakened from the most peaceful sleep I could remember. Last night, we started out on opposite ends of the bed. I woke up in the middle of the night and he was holding me as we laid chest to chest.

By the time I woke up this morning I was laying with my back to his chest with his right arm around my stomach and his left at the top of my head. His fingers were on my scalp. He seemed to be fascinated with my hair.

I stared at him for what felt like forever as he slept. He looked so at ease. His breaths were slow and steady as his chest rose and fell. I couldn't resist the urge to run my fingers down his cheek. Hanif moved slightly, but he didn't wake up.

To keep from touching him anymore I took a shower. By the time I was done he was sitting on the edge of the bed talking to somebody. Must have been his girl because he ended the call when I walked back in.

After he showered and dressed in the same thing he had on yesterday, we went to Waffle House to eat breakfast and talk about what he called my *fucked up situation*. To keep him from worrying about me so much I agreed to see if I could stay with a friend instead of staying in the hotel. Braille's Mom said that I could stay with them... thankfully.

Then he came to pick me up after I finished eating with Braille. He took me back to the hotel and I packed up my things and put them in the car he was letting me use until mine was out of the shop. It was a nice 2014 Mitsubishi Eclipse. He said it was his but he stopped driving it when he bought his new Charger.

I still had no clue what he did for a living. I guess I'd find out eventually. But once I left the hotel I called Elle to see if I could stop by her and Coach Power's crib. By the time I left from speaking with them they both had assured me that Coach Power would get me back in school with no problems as soon as they received my transcript from Cali.

I was glad too because I was only a couple of months away from graduating high school. The last thing I wanted to do was push myself back and have to go for another year. I didn't even want to go for summer school. So I was beyond grateful for him helping me out.

Now I was sitting in Braille's driveway waiting for her to get back home so I could unpack. I met her and Jessica for dinner and bowling, but instead of her coming home at the same time as me, she went to go meet up with some nigga. So I couldn't go in until she got back. The whole time I was with my girls I was thinking about if Hanif was with *his* girl.

I'd started to get used to him already. Yes, I know he's almost ten years older than me and obviously not interested in me... but that didn't keep me from obsessing over him. He probably saw me as a charity case. But that didn't stop my feelings from feeling some type of way. While I waited for Braille to arrive I decided to text Hanif to see if he'd be nice and respond.

He could be so mean sometimes.

But one thing I could say is that he didn't hide it and he was real. I didn't have to wonder about what he was thinking or how he felt. He had no problem letting me know.

Me: *Hanif.*

Mean Old Man: *What?*

Me: *Why you so mean?*

Mean Old Man: *What do you want, Grace?*

Me: *I want you. Where you at?*

Mean Old Man: *What you mean you want me?*

Me: *I mean I miss you. I did spend all today and yesterday practically with you. I miss your company. That's all.*

Mean Old Man: *Oh. I'm at my spot.*

Me: *What spot?*

Mean Old Man: *My business. Didn't I tell you I don't like to be questioned?*

Me: *What kind of business? If you talked like a normal person I wouldn't have to ask you so many questions, Neef.*

Mean Old Man: *Don't give me no nickname. It's a coffee shop during the day and a hookah lounge at night.*

Me: *Why not? And that's dope as hell!*

Mean Old Man: Because that means you're getting comfortable with me. Watch your mouth, little girl. And thanks.

Me: You don't want me to get comfortable with you?

Mean Old Man: *No.*

And with that I cut my car off and sat in the darkness as I waited for Braille to arrive. I hate his ass. Maybe I'd prefer it if he lied. Make my heart feel a little better. Lies would only make me feel worse, though.

Mean Old Man: *Get out your feelings, Grace.*

Me: You're mean.

Mean Old Man: *You've told me that like ten times.*

Me: You need to work on that.

Mean Old Man: *I don't need to work on shit.*

Me: Whatever...

Me: Neef!

Mean Old Man: *. . . .*

Me: Can I come and check your place out?

Mean Old Man: *No.*

Me: Why not?

Braille pulled up on the side of me.

Mean Old Man: *You're too young. You have to be eighteen or older.*

Me: But you know me. I'll be eighteen next month.

Mean Old Man: *Your birthday is April what?*

Me: 29ᵗʰ

Mean Old Man: *You still can't come.*

Braille knocked on my trunk. I popped it and opened my door to grab some of my bags.

Me: Well can I come one morning for a cup of coffee or tea?

I slid my phone in my pocket to avoid dropping it.

"So who did you ditch me to go see?" I asked Braille as we walked to their front door.

"Zo. Lorenzo."

"He go to Kirby?"

"Nah. Melrose."

"Melrose? How you meet him?"

"I had a flat and he helped me. Don't say anything about him in the house. Rule told me I can't talk to him."

"Why not?"

"Because he's a dope boy."

I rolled my eyes and let it go when she unlocked the door. The aroma of home cooked food assaulted my nostrils. I could cook basic stuff. Breakfast, casseroles, and things of that nature. But Ms. Josephine had some soul food going on in her kitchen and I hadn't had any authentic down south soul food since I left.

I couldn't wait to dig in!

We put my bags in their guest room then went to Ms. Josephine's room. She was in the middle of her bed watching TV.

"Hey, baby. Hey, Grace. So glad you're back home."

She got out of her bed and I nodded with a smile.

"Thanks for letting me stay here. I'll be gone by the end of the schoolyear. By the end of the summer at the latest."

"Stay for as long as you need," she offered as she hugged me.

I accepted her warm hug willingly but removed myself to pull the envelope I had for her out of my pocket.

"This is a stack, I mean, one thousand dollars. If you want more just let me know how much and I can pay you monthly."

"Girl please. Put that money in a bank account somewhere. You don't have to pay me a thing. Anything in this house you want or need you help yourself to."

She hugged me again and I felt tears welling up in my eyes.

"Thank you," I mumbled into her shoulder.

"No problem at all, baby. It's some turkey necks, cornbread, and greens on the stove. I made a lemon cake a couple of days ago and it's in there as well."

"Well, I'm still full from dinner, but I wouldn't mind having a slice of that cake."

"Go have at it."

She kissed my forehead and I smiled.

"Thanks, Ms. Josephine. I promise I won't be any trouble."

"Braille, get this girl out of my room. Y'all call me if you need me."

Braille's arm wrapped around mine and she led me to her kitchen. I grabbed a knife while she pulled some French vanilla ice cream out of the freezer.

My phone vibrated in my pocket and I almost dropped the knife trying to get to it.

Mean Old Man: *Fine. You can come for tea. Not tomorrow because I have some shit to do. I'll let you know when. Get you some rest, Grace. And call me if you need me.*

Braille

Our spring break was winding down and I wanted to spend as much time with Lorenzo as I could. He lived in Orange Mound and I lived in East Memphis. I hated driving on the expressway so it took me like thirty minutes to get to his side of town on the streets. I hadn't been to his home yet and I honestly didn't want to, but he was washing his car and told me to bring mine over so he could wash it for me.

I pulled up and it was like twenty niggas hanging around his house. My eyes immediately fell on him. He was standing next to his car shirtless. Smoking on a blunt. Lorenzo nodded my way before slowly making his way to me. I cut my car off and opened the door.

He opened the door wider and grabbed my hand to pull me out of the car and into his arms. The feel of his hands gripping my ass had me blushing as I tried to pull them off.

"I can't touch what's mine?" His eyes were high low as he smiled at me.

"Are you high?"

"Nah. What's up, baby?"

I tried to remove myself from him again but he held me tighter.

"Why you ain't tell me all these people were over here?"

He looked around and shrugged.

"This the hood. Folks just pop up and chill."

"Do you see what I have on? These niggas staring at me and shit. I'm 'bout to go."

Finally, Lorenzo released me and looked at what I had on. Cameron's brother Israel had a clothing store. He created a women's line that his wife Layyah inspired. I was rocking his newest design which was a jersey legging and crop top set. Had I known so many eyes would be on me I wouldn't have worn it.

"The fuck you got this tight ass shit on for, B?"

"Because it's comfortable."

"Man... you blowing my high." Lorenzo turned and looked at the men that were staring at me. "This mine," Lorenzo stated grabbing my arm and pulling me into his side. "She mine. Don't naine one of y'all niggas say shit to her. Don't look at her. Don't even think about her. Any nigga I catch lusting after her I'm putting a bullet between your eyes and that's on my Pops."

One by one the stares stopped and when no one was looking at me anymore Zo released me and went back to his car. I watched as he grabbed his shirt, phone, and keys and made his way back to me.

"I'm about to take your car to the car wash. I wanna talk to you anyway," he mumbled pushing me away from the driver's side of the car.

"Talk to me about what?"

"Just some shit. Us really."

"Us?"

"Yea us."

He opened the passenger door and I got in. Kevin Gates started blasting as soon as he cut my car on and I smiled as he looked at me skeptically.

"What you know about this?"

I was listening to his Luca Brasi 2 mixtape. Knew practically every song and lyric word for word.

"What you mean what I know? What you know?"

Lorenzo cut it up even more and we rapped every song that come on out loud until we pulled up to the car wash. He cut my car off and looked at me with the same look as he did before.

"Why do you keep looking at me like that, Lorenzo?"

"Why do you keep calling me that?"

"That's your name ain't it?"

"Yea, but don't nobody call me that. My mama don't even call me that."

"Well, I ain't your mama. I'll think of you a nickname but it ain't gone be no Zo."

"Why not?"

"Because that's what everybody calls you."

He smiled and got out of the car. After paying to have my car washed, he came and opened my door. We went across the street to this tucked away fish and wing restaurant. I didn't come to the hood on regular occasions because it was such a long drive but whenever I did I made sure to get me some Chinese from Meng's or some catfish from any little cut away spot.

"What you want to eat, B?"

"I don't know. What you getting?"

"They got a three-piece fish plate with two sides and a drink. That's what I usually get. I'm hungry as hell right now, though, so I might get the five-piece."

"Greedy ass. I ain't really that hungry. Just give me a piece of your fish."

"Nah. I'm hungry. I'll just order an extra piece of fish. You sure you don't want nothing?"

"Yea, I'm sure."

Zo looked me up and down then pointed at the table he wanted me to sit at. I sat down and waited for him to place his order. When he sat down, he sat next to me instead of in front of me. I draped my leg over his lap and he grabbed it absently as he looked at the video I was watching on my phone.

"What's that?" His breath on my neck gave me chills.

"A video my sister sent me of my nephew trying to walk."

"He don't look like he's old enough to start walking yet."

I chuckled and smiled proudly.

"He's not. He's only six months. But he's such a busy body."

"Y'all and them gray eyes."

I looked at him briefly and blushed as his arm wrapped around my waist and he pulled me even closer.

"Yea, we got those from my Pops."

"Different mamas?"

"Yep."

"He been there all the time?"

"Nah. I met him a little over a year ago. Right after I met Camryn. I met her first, then she told me about him."

"How did she know y'all had the same daddy?"

"She wasn't sure, but we had the same gray eyes and curly hair. I cut and flat ironed mine, though. So she asked me what my mama's name was and asked our Pops if he knew her. He said yes and that was that."

"He black?"

"White." He rolled his eyes and chuckled. "What's funny?"

"That's why Rule think he gotta pick your boyfriends?"

"That's my brother, and he don't want to pick my boyfriends. He just don't want me to be with you."

"Why the hell not?"

"Because you're a drug dealer."

"What I tell you about that?"

"You are."

"No I'm not."

"What you call it then, LoLo?"

His face scrunched up and I smiled.

"LoLo?"

"Yep. Lorenzo or LoLo. Your choice."

Lorenzo rolled his eyes and I smiled even harder.

"I'm a good man, though. I don't think you should judge me based off how I make my money."

"I'm not. If I was I wouldn't be here." He stared into my eyes and licked his lips. "What about you and your folks? What your mama do? Are your sisters in school or something?"

He took a swig of his tropical punch kool-aid before answering me.

"She's not working right now."

"Why not? Is she sick?"

"I guess you could say that."

His blank expression told me that was something he didn't want to talk about, so I didn't want to pry. I figured he'd tell me in his own timing. But if she wasn't working at all that would explain why he felt the need to put his freedom on the line and sell drugs. I caressed his forearm and kissed his cheek gently.

He smiled and ran his finger down my cheek.

"You're pretty as hell. You know that, Braille?"

"I've heard that a few times."

"Yea I bet."

They called his number and I unwillingly dropped my leg so he could go and get his food. It looked good as hell! For his side's he got fried okra and bbq spaghetti. The cornbread was fresh out of the oven and steaming. I wasn't really hungry… but when I saw his food…

Lorenzo sat down and put my leg back over his lap. We both bowed our heads and said grace. He'd grabbed an extra plate and put my little piece of fish on it. I must have looked the way I felt because he laughed as he opened his tartar sauce.

"Ain't that all you said you wanted?" He asked popping a piece of okra in his mouth.

"But it looks good. Let me taste that okra and spaghetti."

"Man, nah. I told you I was hungry. I'll give you some money and you can go buy you something."

"I don't want no whole plate. Plus, I don't want to wait for it. Just let me taste yours."

He put one piece of okra on my plate and a forkful of spaghetti. Then, he pushed my leg off of him and pushed me closer to the window and away from him and his food.

"Really, Lorenzo? That's how we getting down right now?"

"You better eat before your food gets cold."

"Let me have some, please."

"Nah, man. Told you I was hungry."

I pouted and ate the okra. It was as good as I thought it would be. I scooted closer to him and he shook his head before I even asked for some. Damn. This made me think about my sister and Rule. She was always trying to eat his food. I chuckled at the thought.

"What's funny?"

"Nothing. Just thinking about my sister. She's always trying to eat Rule's food. I used to think she was crazy then but now I understand."

"Understand what?" I shook my head and dipped my fish in his tartar sauce. "Understand what?"

"It's not so much about the food as it is you. Yea it looks and smells good, but… I don't know… I just want it because it's yours. I guess you sharing with me makes me feel like I could trust you with me. Does that make sense?"

"Makes perfect sense." Lorenzo put his plate in the middle of us and I smiled. "Dig in."

Jessica

I woke up this morning to a picture in my inbox on Facebook from Markeda. The picture was of her and Cameron. She was laying on his chest and his arm was wrapped around her. I couldn't see the bottom of them, but neither of them had on shirts.

I started to go to his brother Israel's house and make him take me to Cameron, but Layyah was five months pregnant with their first baby girl together and she's extra live so I didn't want to put them in the middle of it.

So, I decided to call Braille and Grace and see if they wanted to take a road trip to Atlanta. Braille hated driving on the expressway as much as me, so I figured my best bet would be Grace, but I called Braille first anyway.

She answered and laughed into the phone.

"What's up, Jessica?"

"Where you at?"

"In Southaven at the mall with LoLo. Where you at?"

"At home. Tell me why Cameron's so called friend sent me a picture of them in bed together. She was laying on his chest with her bra and shit off and he was sleeping with his arm wrapped around her."

"Are you fucking serious?!" She yelled so loud I had to pull the phone away from my ear.

"Quiet your country ass down," Lorenzo said in the background.

"Girl, yes! I started to call his ass but I don't want him to try and come up with a lie. And I wanna *see* Markeda's ass."

"I feel you. What you wanna do?"

"Road trip."

"You know I'm down. I ain't tryna drive on the interstate, though. You talked to Grace yet? Her grown ass drove all the way here from Cali so I'm sure she wouldn't mind driving."

"I'm about to call her now."

"Okay. Call her and then call me back. I'm about to head to the house. Meet us there. You know she's staying with me now?"

"Right. Right. Aight I'll meet y'all there."

"Okay, boo."

I disconnected the call and called Grace as I paced around my room.

"Hello?"

"Grace, where you at?"

"At the house. What's up?"

"I'm sure this is going to sound weird, but I need you to drive me to Atlanta real fast. We can come right back home unless you want to take a break."

"Okay. For what, though?"

"This bitch sent me a picture of her and my nigga naked hugged up."

"Say no more. You want me to come get you?"

"Nah. I'm about to come over there and wait for B. We can take my car. Gas and food is on me."

"Cool. Well I'm ready when y'all are."

"Aight, thanks."

I hung up and looked at the bear Cameron had given me the first time Markeda caused problems between us. He'd spent the entire day with her and ignored me, then the next day took her to the park while I was at work. It wouldn't have bothered me as much if we didn't go to the park every day when I got off of work and just... talked... for hours.

I told his ass then if he wanted her to leave me the hell alone and be with her, but he said they were just friends.

We're about to see if that's the same story he's going to stick with now.

Lorenzo

I didn't want Braille to know I hated for her to have to leave, but she had to do what she to do. She brought a sense of peace to my life that had been missing since my father died a year ago. His death led to my mama using drugs to numb her pain.

At first it was just cigarettes and liquor. Then it was weed. Then it was crack. Then it was heroin. Now it's anything she can get her hands on. I refuse to let her bring that shit in the house with my little sisters in there. Came home last week and found her sniffing air fresheners through a plastic bag trying to get high.

That was the last straw. I took my sisters and sent them to my grandma's house until my mama was in a position to be a mother. I stayed at the house with her, but I damn near pulled anything out that she could use to get high.

Really all that was left was furniture and clothing. I took all utensils and cleaning supplies out too. She couldn't even cook for herself. Anytime she wanted to eat I was gon' get it for her or have something delivered.

That's really why I hadn't allowed Braille to meet my folks yet. I could tell she was interested in my life and family, but honestly, I was ashamed. I'm sure she thought I was just another nigga out here tryna sell drugs to look cool or hard and live flashy, but I did that shit because it was the quickest way for me to make money to provide for my family.

We had been leaning against her car for a few minutes before I sighed and kissed her forehead. Then her cheeks. I cupped her face with my hand and pecked her lips softly.

"Call me when y'all heading out. And when you get there. And on your way back."

Braille nodded then stood on her tip toes to kiss me again. I smiled and pulled away. I wasn't with all that kissing and shit. Made me too horny. If I wasn't about to smash, I wasn't trying to play with myself like that.

"Boy, you better kiss me. You shouldn't have let me feel them lips," she mumbled wrapping her arms around me.

"Gone on now. I told you I ain't with all that unless I'm about to fuck."

"And I told you I need affection."

"I just gave you a kiss didn't I?"

Her eyes rolled and she sighed heavily as she pushed me away.

"Fine."

"Do as I said, okay?"

"Whatever."

I pulled her into me and kissed her forehead while wrapping her arms back around me.

"You mad?" I whispered into her ear before kissing it.

"Yep."

"We can't have that."

Taking her face into my hands, I parted her lips with mine and kissed her deeper. Longer. Harder. Resisting the urge to slide my tongue into her mouth I pecked her lips a few times before pulling away.

"Will that do?" I released her. Her eyes were closed as she nodded yes. "You still mad?" She shook her head no.

I laughed quietly and opened her door for her.

"Call me, B."

"I will. Be safe, Lorenzo."

"Always."

Braille stood there for a few seconds before getting into her car. I waited until she drove off before getting into my car and driving off.

Grace

B, Jessie, and I looked so out of place. We didn't know where in the hell we were going, but couldn't nobody tell us shit. Jessica's hair was pulled up into a bun. Her side bang was covering the right side of her forehead. She was dressed in black sweats, Nike's, and a baby tee.

Braille was wearing the same outfit in gray. She also had on a gray Grizzlies snapback. I had on a pair of black sweats with a white t-shirt. My hair was in two French braids down my back.

By the time we'd been approached by too many guys to count, Jessie finally asked one of them if he knew who Cameron was. He described him as the light skinned dude with long hair and Jessie told him to show us where he lived.

When we made it to his dorm, Jessie looked from me to Braille. We didn't know when the picture was taken or what we were about to walk into, but we had her back no matter what. I nodded at her and she knocked on the door.

There was no way in the world I could see myself being this possessive of Andy and I was with him for years, but Hanif… I could see myself doing some crazy shit like this over him. And that scared the life out of me. Cameron opened the door and smiled but it fell immediately when Jessica pushed him to the side and walked into his dorm.

"The hell is going on?" He asked.

"Where your bitch at? She here now?" Jessica questioned.

"What are you talking about, Jessie?"

"Markeda! Where she at?"

I closed the door and leaned against it.

"I don't know where she at. I ain't seen her all day. What's going on?"

"You fucking her?"

His eyes lowered. He licked his lips slowly and tilted his head to the side as he stared at her.

"Cameron!"

"Not now. Not since we got back together."

"Then why did she send me a picture of y'all laid up in the bed together this morning?"

"She did what?"

Jessie pulled her phone from her pocket and handed it to him after pressing a few buttons. Cameron stared at the picture for less than a second before handing it back to her.

"That's old," he mumbled taking a step back.

"How old, Cameron?"

"Jessica…"

"How old, Cameron?"

"Last week."

"Last week?!"

"Jessie…"

"You fucked that bitch last week?" He nodded and looked away. "Why?"

"I was horny and she was here."

Jessica did that angry chuckle and took a step back.

"I don't get it. I told you if you wanted her to be with her."

"I don't want to be with her. I want you. You wasn't giving me no play. You just now started acting like this is what you want. I was single when I had sex with her."

"And I'm just supposed to believe that this picture isn't from today?"

"She only sent you that because I told her that we were back together and I couldn't fuck around with her like that anymore, Jessica. Think. Why would I fight as hard as I have for you just to fuck her right after I get you back? Think, baby."

Jessie shook her head and looked away to avoid crying. She looked from Braille to me. I lowered my eyes to keep from seeing the tears in hers.

"Take me to her," she ordered.

"What?"

"You heard me. Take me to her. I want you to end this shit in my face."

"Jessie, there is nothing to end."

"There's not? You think you finna be friends with a bitch that clearly wants to take my spot?"

"So you saying I can't be her friend anymore?"

"That's exactly what I'm saying."

He sighed and put his hands in the pockets of his basketball shorts. Apparently he didn't move as quickly as Jessica wanted him to because she mugged him hard as hell and tried to walk away. Cameron grabbed her arm and stopped her.

"Where you going?"

"Home. I'm not about to play with your ass. If you wanna be her friend that damn bad, be that."

"Listen, you know this ain't that. I'll do what I gotta do to keep you."

"Just... let me go, Cameron. I don't even trust you anymore. I can't believe you've been having sex with her."

Her tears started to fall and I ran my hand over my forehead.

"I'm sorry, okay? But damn it didn't mean shit to me. I love you. I want you."

"That's bullshit. I just told you to let her ass go and you hesitated. If you don't want her why'd you hesitate?"

"Fine."

Cameron released her and went back to his room. He came back with his phone and keys. Grabbing her arm, he led her outside with B and I right behind them.

Jessica rode with him while I trailed behind. Braille and I were silently fuming. I hadn't thought to check my phone since we hit the road hours ago, but Hanif called and since my phone was connected to the Bluetooth in the car when it rang it came up on the dashboard.

I answered with a smile.

"Hey, Neef."

"Where your ass at? I been texting you all day."

"My bad. I'm in Atlanta."

"Atlanta? What for?"

"My homegirl needed to make a quick run down here so I drove."

"A quick run?"

"Yep." He was quiet. Too quiet. I looked over at Braille and she was smiling. "I'm sorry, Hanif, did you need something?"

"Yea, your out of pocket ass."

"What you need me for? I tried to see you yesterday and you were being mean."

"Humble yourself. I got the estimate for your car. It's going to take more to fix it than the car is worth. I'm going to give you the one you're driving now. Meet me at my coffee shop tomorrow morning and I'll sign the title over to you."

Tears were blurring my eyes so bad I had to pull over to the side of the street.

"What did you say?"

"You heard what I said, Grace."

"Why you doing all of this for me?"

"Who else gon' do it for you?"

"Awwww," Braille whined.

"Who is that?"

"My best friend. I got you on Bluetooth in the car. Thanks, Hanif, but you really don't have to give me this car. Just let me pay for it. I can't keep your car."

"I can't drive two at the same time. It's cool. Just meet me here in the morning."

"What time?"

"Ten."

"Okay. Text me the address."

"Okay."

"Hanif?"

"Yea?"

"Thank you."

The line was quiet for a second then he hung up. I wiped my face and sat there as Braille rubbed my back.

"He's... different."

"Yea. I haven't figured him out yet. He's nice and mean at the same time."

"Lovable asshole."

"Basically."

"I think he's only acting like that because he likes you but he doesn't *want* to like you."

I shrugged and got back in traffic.

"Hanif doesn't like me. Call Jessica and see where they are."

"That man loves you, Grace."

"He barely can stand me."

"Whatever. He adores you. He might not want to, but he does." She started talking to Jessica to see where they were. Cameron turned around to find us. The campuses were right next to each other, but we had no idea where she stayed on campus.

"There he is," she mumbled pointing towards his car.

A few minutes later we were parking and getting out of the cars.

"He called her down here," Jessica said walking towards us.

I nodded. At that moment my thoughts were on Hanif and his act of kindness.

No one had ever done something like that for me before, so I really didn't know how to respond. It wasn't because he wanted something in return. He hadn't even tried to see me since I checked out of the hotel. If we talked it was because I called or texted him. I couldn't figure him out at all. That was beginning to mess with me.

We saw four girls walking towards us and I sighed and crossed my arms. I assumed the one in the front was Markeda because she was looking at Cameron smiling.

"What's up, Cammy?" She asked.

Jessica step towards her, but Cameron stepped in front of her.

"Why you send my girl that picture? Why you taking pictures like that of us together anyway?"

"I just thought she needed to know that we were fucking off."

"We *used* to fuck off. I canceled that. Did you forget?" Markeda shrugged and smiled harder. "We can't be friends anymore either. You don't know how to act."

"Whatever, Cammy. You'll be back. You can't get rid of me. If you could you wouldn't be here. Soon as her ass goes back to Memphis you gone be back in my bed."

Jessica ran around Cameron and swung on Markeda. I was never for fighting the person your girlfriend or boyfriend messed around with. The issue was with your mate, not with them, but Markeda was on some disrespectful shit so she deserved whatever Jessica gave her.

And Jessica was giving it to her ass good. She had her on the ground beating the shit out of her ass. One of her friends tried to grab Jessica, and before B or I could check her, Cameron was grabbing her hair and pulling her away from Jessica. Then he grabbed Jessica and pulled her off of Markeda.

"Don't come for me no more, Markeda. You do and I'm gone let her loose on you again," Cameron warned.

I shook my head and walked to the driver's side of the car.

"You think I give a fuck? She only got one on me because I wasn't expecting her ass to jump on me. Try that shit when I'm ready, bitch!"

"Bitch, fuck your weak ass! Stay the hell away from my man! Next time he won't be able to pull me off of you!"

Her friends grabbed her and pulled her away from us. Cameron put Jessica's body on the car and used his to keep her there. When Markeda was out of our sight I opened the door to get inside.

"Can I take you home? We need to talk."

"I ain't got shit to say to you, Cameron."

"You still mad? We weren't together when I had sex with her."

"I know that's supposed to make this okay... but it doesn't. That doesn't stop it from hurting, Cameron. This is why I wanted us to just be friends. So we could do our own thing we were apart and just focus on each other when we were together."

He nodded in understanding.

"But... I want you, though. You done with me?"

"I don't know. I just... need some time to think."

"How much time? Until you get home?"

I smiled and got in the car, but kept the door open so I could be nosey.

"More than that, Cameron."

"Until tomorrow morning?"

"Stop trying to make me laugh. I'm mad at you."

"I'm sorry, Jessie. I love you."

"How can you say you love me but you fucked her?"

"My love for you has nothing to do with what I did with her."

"And that's what scares me. How can I be sure you won't do it again? With her or someone else? I'm not gon' be my sister for you or anyone else."

"I'm not asking you to. I promise I'm not. Just let me take you home so we can talk. Please."

In her silence I heard that she was about to give in.

"Fine." Jessica walked over to me and smiled softly. "Ima ride back with him. Thank y'all."

"It's all love," I mumbled.

She tried to go into her purse to hand me some money but I pushed it away.

"Call me when you get home," we said in unison and smiled.

"I think we're going to stop and eat and maybe go to the mall before we go home so you'll probably get there first," I said.

"Yea, but Cam's ass gon' have her hemmed up for some makeup sex," Braille mumbled. Her eyes never left her phone.

"No he ain't. He ain't getting none of this for a good little minute."

"That's a lie. I can have it right now if I wanted it," Cameron said pulling her away from the car. "Y'all be safe. Memphis got some crazy drivers but they don't have nothing on these folks here in Atlanta."

"I see." I grabbed the door handle. "Alright, boo. We'll talk later."

Jessica nodded and they walked over to his car. I looked over at Braille and she stopped texting Lorenzo long enough to look at me.

"You think she gon' forgive him?" She asked me.

I cranked up the car and shrugged.

"Yep. That's not the question. The question is going to be if she makes his ass pay for this over and over and over again."

She nodded as she cut the Kendrick Lamar we were listening to up.

Hanif

Why was I nervous as I waited for Grace to arrive? She made me nervous. She made me feel. I *hated* feeling. I was starting to care about her and I hated caring about people because I always lost those I cared about.

There were things about me and my past that I didn't want her to know about. Things that would help her understand why I handled her the way I did, but I refused to let her in on those things.

When I was a young nigga, I was known on the streets as Savage. I was a hood star. I rapped and sold drugs trying to make it out the hood. One night while I was doing a show, the chick that I was dating at the time used her connection with me to get backstage. She was hired by a nigga named Red to rob me, but my brother caught her.

They killed him.

I've carried that weight around with me for the past six years.

It's because of that that I don't trust women. I don't trust niggas. I don't trust nobody besides my family. After my brother was murdered I fell into a deep depression. I stopped rapping but I didn't quit writing poetry. The drugs were no more. I invested in a couple of businesses to set up a residual income and opened my coffee shop / hookah lounge.

To this day, I still don't know where Red is. When I saw the surveillance tape and saw Red and Ciara together I went on a killing spree. I killed her and every one of Red's family member's I could get my hands on hoping he'd man up and give his life for theirs but he never did.

Before I lost my brother I lost my best friend Trent. He was taken from us by a jealous thieving ass fraud that wanted to take what Trent had instead of trying to work for it.

Before him it was my high school girlfriend. She was killed by a drunk driver a week before our prom. I couldn't go. Couldn't even finish the schoolyear. I ended up having to go to summer school just to graduate.

So yea. I guard my heart ferociously these days. The only reason I kept Pria around on a consistent basis is because I don't believe in sleeping around with too many different women at the same time. She's my main chick. The only one that knows where I lay my head at night. But she's never met my family and I plan on keeping it that way.

There's no future for us. Just present companionship.

Then there's Olivia and Ava. I fuck around with them when Pria pisses me off or when she's on her period.

But Grace... Grace makes me want to open up. She makes me want to share. Talk. Be affectionate. That night at her hotel room I... I held her. And I didn't want to let her go. That's not me. I don't even hold Pria. She's never even spent the night at my house.

But Grace... this young troubled girl... is waking my heart up and I swear I'm trying to keep this beast asleep.

Grace walked into my shop and looked around for me. When her eyes landed on me she smiled and walked towards me. I hated that I loved everything about her. Her eyes. Her hair. Her melanin. Her shape. The way she mumbles when she sleeps. How she crinkles her nose when she doesn't like what I'm saying. How she sneezes that cute little sneeze when she's been outside for too long and her allergies start acting up.

I stood and went to my office to grab the title for the car. I can't explain why I was doing all for her that I was. I just... felt obligated to. When I walked back out she was seated. Picking up pieces of her hair and running her hands down it.

That was supposed to be my job.

I sat across from her and she smiled.

"Did you have fun in Atlanta?" I asked while sliding the title over to her.

She shrugged as she placed her elbows on the table.

"It was cool. Hanif..."

"Don't start, Grace. The title is already signed over to you. It's yours."

"I just don't understand why."

Her voice was so low as she lowered her head. I'd learned anytime she did that she was getting emotional and trying not to cry.

"Why does there have to be a reason why?"

"People don't just give people cars, Hanif. They don't just offer to get people's cars fixed. They don't..." She ran her hands down her face and shook her entire body.

"What do you want me to say, Grace?" Damn. My voice almost sounded desperate.

"I want you to tell me that you want to have sex with me. That you have a fetish for young girls. That I remind you of your sister. Of your child. That you're a secret relative that I know nothing about. Something. Something to make this make sense."

I smiled softly and ran my fingers down my chin. *She had no idea how I felt about her.*

"Grace…" The bell on my door chimed. I looked up and groaned at the sight of Pria. "We'll talk later," I mumbled as I stood.

Pria opened her mouth to say some slick shit but I held my hand up and silenced her. She remained quiet as I pointed towards my office for her to go in there and meet me.

"Let me walk you out," I offered.

"That's her?"

"Who?"

"You know who, Hanif."

For some reason… it sounded different when she said my name that time.

"Yea, that's her."

"She's pretty. She fits you."

"What that mean?"

Grace shrugged and remained silent. I opened the door and she walked to her car a few steps ahead of me. She tried to open it but I shut it.

"Get out your feelings, Grace." She nodded but avoided my eyes. I used my hand to lift her head. Her hand covered my wrist as she stared back at me. "You're so young."

"I get it," her voice was low as she pushed my hand away.

I opened her door and she got inside.

"You really don't, but I guess it's best this way."

"No I guess I don't because you don't know how to use your words."

I started to tell her that she was wrong. That I *chose* not to use my words. That I had notebooks of poetry that said otherwise. The most recent of which had been about her.

"Don't keep your girl waiting for long, Hanif."

My girl is sitting right here in front of me.

"Fine, Grace. So I guess you won't be texting me anymore since you're in your feelings, huh?"

"You ain't been wanting to talk to me anyway. Get the hell off my car so I can go."

I smiled and shook my head.

"So, it's your car now?"

"Yea, you wanna take it back?"

"Nah. You don't have to worry about anything I give you being returned."

She nodded and started the car.

Why was it so hard for me to let her go?

"Neef…"

"Goodbye, Grace. Be safe."

"Goodbye?"

I nodded and closed her door. She sat there for a second. As if she was trying to register what I said. This was goodbye… at least until her eighteenth birthday.

Braille

When I talked to Lorenzo this morning he seemed distant and distracted. Like he had a lot on his mind. I asked him what was going on and he told me nothing... but I knew something was up. So, since it was Sunday and I'd be heading back to school tomorrow I wanted to do something special for him and spend a little more time with him.

I pulled up at his house and I heard screaming from inside. The front door was wide open. I looked around and there were people standing around looking, pointing, laughing, and shaking their heads. Slowly, I got out of my car and pulled the cupcakes and teddy bear I bought him from the passenger's seat.

As I walked up to the front door the woman I guessed was his mother came out with the most deranged look on her face. Lorenzo came out right behind her with anger sketched on his. He was so caught up in her that he didn't notice me standing there. Until she rushed towards me and grabbed the cupcakes from my hands.

"Is it in here? Did you get her to hide it from me? Is she in on it too?" She asked in one breath as she crumbled the cupcakes.

Lorenzo grabbed her arm and flung her on the opposite side of him and away from me. He was yelling at her as she clawed at his hands to get out of his grip... but his words weren't registering in my head. I was too busy trying to process what the hell I'd just walked into. Looking around at the onlookers it hit me.

His mother was on something. Something that gripped her tightly.

"What the hell are you doing here? Didn't I tell you not to come over here unless I told you to?" Lorenzo growled at me.

I watched as his mother ran down the street. He grabbed my chin and forced me to look at him.

"You sounded... I wanted... I'm sorry." His face softened as he released mine. I took a step back and pulled my keys from my purse. "I'm sorry. I'll go."

"No. Don't leave me."

Lorenzo turned and walked back into his home and I sluggishly followed behind him. The outside of his home looked like an ordinary small house in the hood, but the inside was the complete opposite. It was full and spacious. Beautifully furnished, but that's about all that was there. No entertainment electronics and appliances. There were pictures leaning against the walls instead of hanging up that were cracked.

He led me up two sets of stairs to a floor that had only one bedroom on it. A bedroom with an iron door. I'd never seen that before. When he opened the door music immediately filled my ears as smoke blurred my eyes.

His room looked just like I thought it would. He had a huge flat screen TV with multiple gaming consoles attached to it. Posters of sports greats lined his walls along with two young girls and an older couple. One of the people on the picture was the lady that had just ran off. In the picture she looked healthy. Happy. Young. Vibrant. And the older man looked just like Lorenzo. Well, I guess Lorenzo looked just like his Father.

There was a small microwave and mini fridge in the corner. He walked over to it and grabbed a bottle of Hennessey before lowering the volume on his music. I scratched my scalp and watched as he stretched across his king sized bed.

"Get over here," he mumbled.

I sat on the edge of the bed with my back to him. Out of the corner of my eye I saw him take a long gulp of the Hen. He placed it on the floor next to his bed then pulled me back and onto his chest.

"Take this off, please. I need to feel closer to you." Lorenzo tugged at my shirt.

Sitting up, I looked down and into his saddened eyes as I ran my fingers across his cheek. He pulled his shirt over his head and my fingers lowered to his tatted chest and six pack.

"B... please..."

I pulled my shirt over my head but kept my sports bra on. He pulled me back down to him and I caressed his chest.

"I guess you see why I'm in the streets now. She can't take care of my sisters. She can't even take care of herself."

"Where are your sisters?"

"At my grandma house. I sent them there when I saw that her habit was getting worse."

"Lorenzo, you can't save her. She needs professional help. My best friend, Jessica, the one we went to Atlanta with... her sister was on drugs too. She was so heartbroken over a nigga that she used drugs to make her pain go away. She overdosed. Left her baby in the care of her mother. I'm not saying that's going to happen to your mother, but you can't save her. She needs help. You need help. You can't handle this on your own."

Instead of answering me he flipped me onto my back and looked down at me. I ran my hand down his shoulder and arm. Lorenzo held my hand and kissed me softly. When his tongue slid into my mouth I flinched from my surprise. He'd never given me the tongue before. Said he didn't do that unless he was about to have sex.

His body hovered over mine as he spread my legs with his knees. My hands went down his chest and gripped his waist as he continued to kiss me deeply. Slowly. Gently. But with enough pressure to make my inner thighs wet.

"I know this ain't what you came over here for, but I need you," he whispered into my neck before sucking it and biting down on it gently.

I shivered and wrapped my legs around his waist. Lorenzo stopped immediately and stared down at me.

"Is this... you're not a virgin... are you?"

I wanted to lie. I wanted to tell him that I wasn't. Because I didn't want him to stop. I wanted him to dry the river he'd created between my thighs. I wanted to make him feel better in any way that I could.

"B..."

"Yes."

He lifted himself a little further before running his fingers down my pussy. I wrapped my legs around him tighter. Hoping he wouldn't pull away.

"This can't be your first time. I want it to be special."

"But it's fine, LoLo. I promise I don't mind."

Lorenzo smiled softly then bit down on his lip.

"Did I get you wet?"

Without waiting for me to answer him, Lorenzo pulled the basketball shorts I had on down. As he looked into my eyes he removed my panties and spread my legs. I closed my eyes until I heard him suck in breath. His fingers slid between my bottom set of lips and I moved against him involuntarily.

He pulled his finger from me and the sight of my juice on his finger and hanging from me fascinated me.

I'd never been *that* wet before.

Lorenzo put his finger into his mouth and sucked my juice away. I licked my lips and ran my hands down my face.

"You want me to take care of that, baby?"

I nodded adamantly and he smiled as he lowered his face between my legs. The first feel of his tongue against my flesh had me closing my legs and gripping his head. Quickly, I pulled my hand away and lifted my arms over my head.

He looked up at me while he sucked on my clit and grabbed my arms. After putting my hands back on his head he squeezed my breasts and circled my nipples with his middle fingers.

Between his nibbling, licking, and sucking I was moaning, shaking, and coming within a few minutes. He blew on my clit and moaned as I tried to settle down from my orgasm. My first orgasm. And that caused me to jerk even harder. And that caused him to latch back onto my clit. It was so tender I pushed him away and tried to compose myself.

My shaking stopped. My breathing returned to normal. My eyes opened fully. He stood and went into the bathroom that connected to his bedroom. Lorenzo returned with a wet towel and wiped the remains of my insides from my legs.

"You can take a shower when you feel up to it," he mumbled sitting on the side of the bed. "B?"

"Yea?"

"I'm yours. And you're mine. I'm here to please you. So if you want to grab my head do that shit. You wanna squeeze me, choke me, hold me… whatever you wanna do you can do. It's my job to please you. Don't hold back. Don't be scared."

I smiled and sat up so that our faces were just a few inches apart. My fingers slid down his spine softly.

"What does this mean, Lorenzo?"

"It means I'm your nigga and you're my girl."

I blushed and lowered my gaze before returning my eyes to his.

"So that means it's my job to please you too?"

64

"Pleasing you pleased me, Braille. I'm good."

My hand lowered until it found his still hard dick.

"Doesn't feel like you're pleased. You made me feel good. I want to make you feel good too."

"What you wanna do?" His eyes lowered. His voice was so husky it made chills occupy my skin. It made my nipples harden.

"Feed me, boy," I mumbled into his lips before kissing them.

Lorenzo grabbed a handful of my hair and I moaned as he pulled me down onto the bed and covered me.

"You sure?"

"I'm positive."

He stood and removed his boxers. I looked between his thighs and began to regret my decision. There was no way I was going to be able to fit all of him in my pussy let alone in my mouth, but I was damn sure going to try.

We heard the faint sound of a door closing and he shut his eyes tightly.

"Zo!" His Mother yelled. Her feet began to climb the stairs.

I stood and kissed his neck. His arms wrapped around me. His face went into my neck. My hands caressed his back up and down.

"ZO!" She yelled at the same time that she banged against his bedroom door. "You tell these little corner boys not to sell to me? ME! Your fucking mama? I gave you life! You gon' let them deny me? ME!"

I took his face into my hands and stared into his watering eyes. The sight made mine water.

With a lowered voice she said, "Baby, please. Help Mama out. Just this one last time. Just this one last time and I promise I'll stop. I'll stop, okay? Right… right after this."

His eyes began to leak and I quickly wiped his tears away. When I had his face dry he removed himself from me and grabbed his computer.

After handing it to me he said, "Can you look up some rehab facilities for me?"

"Anything you need."

"ZO!" The yelling and beating began again.

His hand covered my neck, lifting my head slightly. He kissed me and rested his forehead on mine. I kissed his cheek and wrapped my free arm around him.

"I'm here," I mumbled into his lips.

"Thank you."

We locked eyes for a second before he left his room to deal with his mother. I sat in the middle of his bed, took a deep breath, and turned his laptop on. Before doing my search I shot my mama a text and told her I'd be a few more hours. There was no way I could leave him. Not like this. Not right now.

Lorenzo

I hated that Braille had to see my mother and me in that condition, but I was glad she was there yesterday. The thought of checking my mother into rehab had never crossed my mind. I guess I thought my tough love and control would be enough to help her shake her habit. But it wasn't enough. I wasn't enough. It was like… her love for her high overshadowed her love for herself and her own children.

She agreed to go to rehab surprisingly, so we signed her up for a six-month program. I wasn't sure if she'd stay the entire length of the program, but that's what a nigga had been praying for all morning.

After I dropped her off I went to pick up my little sisters, Ladia and Chelsea. Of course my grandma questioned me about how I planned on taking care of them with my mother being gone. Shit… the same way I'd been taking care of them while she was here!

As I looked over at Ladia in the passenger seat of my car I couldn't help but smile. She looked so much like my mother. All I could do was pray that she didn't love just as hard yet weakly as my mother did. I told my O.G. Rule about my mama's situation and he told me to get up with him so we could talk about it.

He'd always been a philosophical, deep nigga, but ever since he started graduate school to become a Counselor he was really playing the hood therapist. Even though I knew he didn't want me to try to get at B, now seemed like the best time to tell him that we were kicking it.

I dropped Ladia and Chelsea off at my cousin Simone's beauty shop then headed to Rule's crib.

Me and Braille were pulling up at the same time. I walked over to her and opened the door for her. Pulling her into my arms, I held her close since she was trying to get out of a nigga's grip.

"Stop, LoLo. They might be looking."

"So?"

Braille looked up at me and softened my heart. I released her unwillingly. If she wanted me to keep my hands to myself until we told Rule and her sister about us I guess I could give her that.

"Cam probably in the backyard with them damn animals," Braille mumbled more to herself than me as we walked to the front door.

"Animals?"

"Yea. She's got a whole bunch of shit in the backyard. Horses, cows, pigs, chickens. She's into that shit. She grows a lot of their fruit and vegetables too."

"Word? That's cool."

"Yea, she probably gon' have you leaving here with bags full of food to take home."

"Shit, that's fine with me. Ain't nothing like some fresh fruit and vegetables. Especially if you gon' come over and make a meal out of it."

Braille smiled and knocked on the door. A few seconds later Rule was opening. He was smiling, but when he saw me standing behind her his smile fell.

"Thought I told you she was off limits?" He questioned as he opened the door wider for us to walk in.

"I'm sorry. I couldn't help it. Just something about her."

"You hurt her or get her caught up in some shit... I'll kill you. You know I don't play."

"I know. I'll take full responsibility."

Braille looked from him to me – unsure of how to respond to our exchange. I kissed her forehead and pushed her slightly.

"Can you go kick it with your sister for a minute so I can rap with him?" I asked, closing the door behind us.

"She in the back?" Braille asked Rule.

"You already know. Got my son out there tryna milk cows and everything."

We smiled and Braille went in one direction while he led me to another. Rule and I made it to what I figured was his man cave and he offered me a hit of the blunt he'd just lit. I took a puff and leaned back in my seat.

"So, what's up? Did your mama go?"

I handed him the blunt back and nodded.

"Yea, thank God. When I stepped to her about it last night I really didn't expect her to agree. Not this soon at least, but she seemed like she really wanted to be helped."

"That's good. You say she started using right after your pops died?"

"Yep. I guess that was her trigger. She loved that man with all of her heart."

"That's the problem. We out here loving people with all of our hearts and following our hearts like that motherfucker ain't reckless."

I leaned forward.

"Explain."

"Your heart doesn't consider the consequences of pursuing what it wants. It's irrational. It wavers. It's inconsistent. It's based on feelings. Feelings that change. Your heart is selfish. It can be hypocritical. Judgmental. The bearer of ulterior motives. Your heart must be guarded and protected to function properly. That's why God offers to give us a clean heart.

I knew a man who killed himself after his wife died. He loved her that much that he just couldn't take living without her. His family justified the shit. Talking about he just loved her so much, but that wasn't healthy. Because our hearts are the seat of our emotions, when our emotions change, it effects our heart. Our health.

Stressing and being heartbroken can literally make you sick physically. Mentally. It can have you thinking so one sided and believing you'll never be able to shake that heartache. That grief. I'm not saying that you should completely ignore your heart, but you need to have balance. Your mama didn't have balance. Then she's a woman so she's already more in tune with her heart and emotions than her brain and logic. You just have to be balanced."

"How? How do you balance yourself?"

"As my wife would put it, by loving God, yourself, and then others. You can't love another human being more than you love yourself. You can love them as much as or like you love yourself, but the only being that you should love more than yourself is God.

That's where the balance comes in. *It's not about being selfish; it's about keeping the right perspective. Putting you first doesn't mean you value them less. It means you value them as you value yourself.*

You won't hurt them because you won't hurt yourself. You won't lie to them because you won't lie to yourself. You won't disrespect them because you won't allow yourself to be disrespected. Loving self has gotten such a bad rap, but you really can't fully love another person unconditionally until you've learned to love yourself.

You can love people in a healthy way only when you love yourself in a healthy way. At the end of the day, this life won't last forever. Death is a part of life, and when you love people more than you love yourself..."

"When they die or leave you, you end up destroyed mentally and emotionally because of the weight you placed on them for love."

"Exactly. So rehab is cool. It's a *damn* good start. It will get her clean physically. Then you'll have to make sure she gets some help mentally, emotionally, and spiritually. You know I'll help with that in any way that I can."

I nodded and leaned back in my seat.

"I 'preciate you," I mumbled.

"It's cool. You remind me of me in my younger days. I got out. Get out the streets before it's too late. You won't be doing your mama, your sisters, or Braille any good behind bars."

I stood. He stood. We shook up and went outside where the girls were. Braille was in her own little world playing with her nephew and I smiled. Yea, the streets didn't love nobody, but as of now, they were being mighty good to me.

Jessica

We've been back in school for a month. Cam and I are doing pretty good. He was going to be home this weekend for his brother Israel and my sister Layyah's baby shower. He comes to visit me as much as he can, and I appreciate all the effort he invests in us… but I don't know. It feels so serious. So mature. So eternal. It feels like I'm saving myself for him when he's not around and I'm getting over that.

I'm young. I want to enjoy my life. That's what I wanted for Cam but he just *had* to be in a committed relationship with me. There's no doubt that I love him and appreciate him but I'm just not on the same level as him.

I don't want to be tied down at this point in my life. But he's such a good guy. I'd be a fool to let him go. I guess I really just hate the fact that he's not here with me. I think it would be okay if he was here, but with us being so far away and me having to watch Braille and Lorenzo be all lovey dovey… it's just irritating.

Grace's birthday was a couple of days away, so B and I were at the mall looking for something to buy her. I got her a flat iron from a kiosk we passed and two PINK sweat sets from Victoria's Secret. Braille got her a pair of Curry's and some Nike leggings that were the same shade of blue.

She was hungry so we stopped at the food court and I groaned when Lorenzo walked up on us.

I hung my head and she asked, "What's wrong?"

"Your boyfriend," I mumbled taking a sip of my drink.

Braille turned around and smiled widely at the sight of Lorenzo. It was so cute I couldn't help but smile. He grabbed her neck and pulled her up. They kissed and I rolled my eyes.

"Don't be like that. I can give you some affection if you want me to."

I looked to the left of Lorenzo to see who was talking to me. I hadn't even paid his friend any attention until he spoke. He was cute in a rough kind of way. The complete opposite of Cameron.

His skin was the shade of almonds. His lips were full and smooth as hell. They were almost the same shade of his skin. He smiled and graced me with a pretty white smile along with four gold caps on his teeth. There were two on each side at the bottom of his mouth. But they weren't in the center like most people wear them. They were off to the side and visible only when he really smiled.

Sexy as hell.

His eyes were coffee brown, slightly slanted, and tight. He had the kind of eyes that made his stare deep and penetrative. I smiled even though I didn't want to and returned my attention to my drink.

"You hear me, Beautiful?"

I looked up at him again and shook my head. *Why couldn't I think of anything to say?*

"Jessica, you wanna walk around with them for a little while or you ready to go?" Braille asked.

"I'm ready to go. Zo can't take you home?"

"Yea, I'll take her."

"Cool."

I stood and grabbed my purse from the back of my chair, then reached for my bags but ole boy grabbed them and pulled them from my reach.

"So you're ignoring me?" He asked as I reached for my bags, but he held them higher.

"Just talk to the nigga, Jessie. He gon' annoy you until you do," Lorenzo warned me while wrapping his arms around Braille.

"I'm sorry. What did you say?" I asked him finally.

"I told you that I could give you some affection if you wanted me to."

"No thanks. May I have my bags back, please?"

He smiled. I smiled.

"If I give them to you you're going to leave." It sounded like he was telling me instead of asking me. I didn't know how to respond so I nodded. "Well I ain't giving them to you yet. What's your name, Beautiful?"

"In a relationship," I mumbled reaching for the bags again.

"Are you married?"

"Nah."

"Then you're still available. What was your name?"

"Jessica."

"It's nice to meet you, Jessica. I'm Vega." Vega held his hand out for me. I bit down on my lip and timidly put my hand inside of his.

"Wish I could say the same."

Vega smiled and pulled me closer to him.

"You saying it's not nice to meet me?"

"Not at all. I'm trying to leave and you're holding my bags hostage."

"Let me get your number."

"I'm not interested."

"Then why are you smiling?"

"I just like to smile."

"You weren't smiling before I got over here."

"Yes I was."

"Yea you were, but it fell, which brings me back to my original proposition..."

"No. Will you give me my bags?"

"Vega, give my sister her bags so she can go. LoLo, make him give her the bags." B tried to help me, but neither of them were taking her seriously.

I wrapped my arms over my chest and put most of my weight on my right side. He looked me over and shook his head.

"You sexy as hell. Your dude treating you right?"

"He treats me very well, thank you."

"I can treat you better."

He was cocky. *Why did I like that?*

"How do you know?"

"Try me." Vega handed me my bags and licked his lips. "So you gone try me or not?"

"Not."

I turned to walk away but stopped when I felt him behind me. My feet stopped moving and I turned around to find him looking me up and down. His eyes met mine and he smiled.

"Where you going, Vega?"

"I'm walking you to your car."

"I don't need you to walk me to my car."

"But you want me to."

"No the hell I don't."

"The quicker you let me walk you out the quicker you can give me your number and I can leave."

I laughed, but it wasn't a *haha* laugh. It was an *I know this nigga didn't* laugh. Like... what part of I have a boyfriend didn't he understand?

"What part of I have a boyfriend don't you understand?"

"What part of I don't give a fuck don't you understand? I take what I want." Vega paused and looked me over again. "I want you."

Taking a step back I put some space between us and looked behind him to Lorenzo and Braille. He was shaking his head while she was smiling. Like she didn't know I had a boyfriend. If I knew her as well as I thought I did, she was probably thinking about us double dating and kicking it as a group.

"Your pursuit is cute, but I'm not interested, Vega."

"You not?"

He took a step towards me. I took a step back.

"I'm not."

"You're lying, but if you want to play this game that's cool. Let me be a gentleman and walk you out, though."

I didn't trust his ass but I figured this would be the easiest and quickest way to get out of this damn mall. To give him a bit of what he wanted. We walked to my car in silence. I popped my trunk and put her stuff back there just in case she got in my car before I had a chance to take it out.

"Jess..." Vega spoke in a low tone.

I turned to face him slowly after I closed my trunk.

"Yes, Vega?"

"Let me have you."

The walls of my pussy literally throbbed. I couldn't explain what it was about him. The way he looked at me and talked to me. But he was taking me to a place Cameron never had before. How could he pull this type of reaction out of me physically when I was trying so damn hard to resist him mentally?

"I already belong to someone."

"Nah... he's just renting you right now. You belong with a nigga like me. You know how I know?"

My lips partly slightly as I leaned against my trunk. I felt my head shake no but I remained silent.

"Because if you were mine I'd have your mind so gone there wouldn't be anything another nigga or anybody else could say to make you give him some play."

What was I supposed to say to that?

It didn't matter. He didn't give me a chance to reply. He just… walked away. I stood there for a few seconds. Trying to compose myself and talk myself out of walking back in there at the same time. When I felt like myself I got in the car and pulled my phone out of my purse to charge while I drove. I hadn't even made it out of the parking lot before I was getting a call from B.

"What's up, B?"

"This ain't Braille. This your future baby daddy."

My mouth smiled. My heart dropped. My eyes closed. I opened them immediately when I remembered I was driving.

"What do you want, Vega?"

"You. I just wanted to let you know that I'm getting your number out of B's phone since you giving me such a hard time. I'll hit you up tonight when I get home and settled. So when you see an unknown number hit you up answer cause it's me."

"Nigga, don't you get my number out of that girl's phone."

He laughed then hung up without saying anything. I groaned and damn near chunked my phone back into the cup holder.

But why was I still smiling, though?

Cameron

Of course I had to come home for Israel and Layyah's baby shower. They were going to name my niece Isabell. She would be Israel's second child and Layyah's first. I still can't believe their crazy asses settled down and finally committed to each other… but I was glad they did.

That's how me and Jessie met. Layyah's sister Alayziah knew Jessica first because she dated Jessica's brother. Then Jessica met Layyah. Then that shit went down with her sister's ex and they decided they were going to help her come out of her shell. So they introduced us to each other.

It was supposed to be a little summer time fling but shit got real. At least for me it did. Sometimes I wonder about Jessie. I know she cares about me, and she says she loves me, but I just don't know if she's as invested in this as I am.

It seems as if what happened to her sister has shaped her so much that she avoids really getting close to me at all costs. I thought when she committed to me again that that would change. Only difference now is that I come home more to kick it with her. I don't know. *Maybe I'm tripping.*

Jessica walked over to me and kissed me quickly before sitting next to me.

"Hey, baby. How long have you been here?" She asked me.

"A couple of hours. I called you."

"Oh."

I chuckled and readjusted myself in my seat.

"What's up, Jessica?"

"What you mean?"

"You're dry as hell."

"I'm just tired. I was up late. You know Grace's birthday is in a couple of days. I was at the mall all day with B looking for something for her. That sun had me drained when I got home."

I nodded and looked away from her. Her hand covered mine and she stuck her fingers between mine.

"I love you," she whispered into my neck.

I looked at her and nodded.

"I love you too, Jessie."

Her eyes looked like there was something on her mind. Something that she wanted to say. If she didn't want to tell me... it was probably something I didn't want to hear. So instead of asking her what was up I just sat back in my seat and sighed. Shit was gon' have to change. Soon.

Grace

I woke up this morning to a Facetime request from Hanif. I hadn't heard from him since he signed his car over to me. Not because I didn't want to... but because I was tired of feeling like I liked and wanted a man that wanted nothing to do with me romantically.

Once I was done wiping my eyes and licking my lips I ran my fingers through my hair since I'd been too lazy to wrap it the night before and accepted his request.

"Took you long enough. Happy birthday, Grace."

A smile covered my face even though I was trying my hardest to keep it in.

"Thank you, Neef. I'm surprised you remembered."

"So, what do you want?"

My smile fell as I looked at him skeptically.

"What do I want?"

"For your birthday."

My smile returned.

"You calling is enough, Hanif." He stared at me in silence. "Neef..."

"I miss you."

"What?"

"You heard me."

"Say it again."

He licked his lips and smiled softly.

"I miss you, Grace."

"I know what I want for my birthday now."

"What's that?"

"You."

"Grace..."

"Just your companionship, Neef. And your undivided attention. And for you to actually open up to me. And answer all of my questions."

I waited for him to say no like the meanie he is but he nodded.

"I can give you that."

My mouth opened slightly from my surprise. His smile widened and I couldn't help but smile. It was so big and beautiful it literally lit up his whole face.

"You have a beautiful smile, Hanif. You should do it more often."

"What time will you be ready, Grace?"

"I don't know. Maybe in an hour. Are you going to feed me?"

"Don't I always? Text me the address to where you are. I'll be there in an hour."

My words left me so I nodded and ended the call. He knocked me off my square. I refused to let him put me in my feelings again, so I had to use this hour to reposition myself.

Hanif

I'm sure Grace wanted to kill me. I told her I was going to scoop her up in an hour. That was at nine this morning. Now it was close to seven in the evening and I was just now pulling up to where she was staying. I didn't plan on taking so long, but the young lady that was supposed to work the day shift at my coffee shop called in. I could've gotten someone to cover her shift, but I needed to get my mental together.

Grace was about to unlock some shit inside of me that hadn't been opened in years. She didn't trip about me taking longer. She just got up with her friends and did her thing with them while she waited for me.

I walked up to her door and knocked. Either I was nervous and impatient or it took forever for somebody to open the door. Grace opened the door and I had to take a step back to take her in. Her hair was in loose curls, and her face looked like it was glowing naturally. Her lips were painted the same plum color as the knee length form fitting dress she had on.

Looking down at the pumps she had on caused me to wonder how they'd look wrapped around my neck. To keep my thoughts from roaming I handed her the purple lilies I'd gotten her.

"My favorite color. Thank you, Hanif." She put them to her nose and inhaled them. "Give me a second to put these in some water and I'll be right out."

I nodded and went back to my car. A short while later she was walking back out of the house and locking up behind her. When I opened the door for her I was close enough to take in her scent. She smelled and looked good as hell.

"You look beautiful, Grace."

"Well aren't you being nice tonight. Thank you."

I pushed her into the car softly and got in myself. The ride to Flight was silent for the most part. We chatted a little during dinner. It wasn't until I took her back to my place that we actually started talking. My Beats Pill was playing some smooth and low shit in the background. A few Soy candles were lit here and there.

She'd taken her shoes off and was laying on my couch by time I changed into a pair of basketball shorts. I blushed as she looked my chest over. When I was in the house I hardly wore anything. Had she not been here I wouldn't have even had on these shorts.

I handed her one of my shirts to put on so she could feel more comfortable.

"You're... very... fit," she mumbled quickly before leaving the living room and going to the bathroom.

I chuckled and grabbed us two bottles of water. She came back looking even more relaxed than she had before.

"Okay, let's get this over with," I said before drinking some water.

Grace rolled her eyes and sat next to me. "Why don't you like talking about yourself?"

I shrugged and watched as she turned sideways to face me.

"I just don't."

"How can you be in a relationship with someone that you don't relate to?"

Impressed... I turned slightly as well.

"What I have with Pria isn't about relating."

"Then what is it about?"

"Sex. And normalcy."

"Tell me about you. Give me the basics."

"My name is Hanif Patterson. I'm twenty-six years old. Gemini. My birthday is June sixteenth. I was born in Baltimore, but my family moved here when I was five. My pops is from here and his Mother was sick so he wanted to be closer to her. I was... a little wild nigga in my younger days. Sold drugs. Rapped. Got it by any means."

"I thought you looked familiar. Savage!" I hung my head and licked my lips. "I remember listening to your CD when I was like twelve."

"God, that makes me feel so fucking old."

She smiled and gripped my forearm.

"Don't start. Keep going. Why did you stop rapping?"

I sighed heavily and scratched my nose.

"At my last show my brother was murdered. I was dating this chick named Ciara. Come to find out she was working for this nigga that hated my ass named Red. His plan was to have her as his way in to hit me up. They tried to get in my dressing room while I was performing, but my brother was back there. He confronted them and Red shot him."

"I'm so sorry for your loss."

I nodded and removed my arm from her grasp.

"Is that why you don't like opening up to people? Because you don't trust them?"

"That's part of the reason. Just seems like those closest to me die. He was murdered. My best friend was murdered. My high school sweetheart was killed by a drunk driver. Right before our prom. That shit fucked with me tough. I'd seen niggas die in the streets before... but losing her... losing her did something to me."

Grace lowered her head. I looked over at her and took her hand into mine. She looked up at me and smiled with half of her mouth.

"Get out your feelings, Grace."

"You still love her?"

"I guess I always will."

"That's understandable, but you can't close your heart off to love just because of what you've lost, Hanif."

"Is that it for your questions?"

She stared at me for a few seconds before removing her hand from mine.

"This is a waste of time. You're never going to let me in."

"The fuck do you think I'm doing, Grace?"

"How? How are you going to let me into your heart when you're reserving it for a person who isn't even here anymore? Loyalty is for the living, Hanif. Ain't shit she can do for you from the grave."

Grace stood and began to pace in front of me. The fifth time she passed me I grabbed her hips and stopped her.

"I'm sorry. That came out way harsher than I wanted it to."

My hands moved from her hips down to her thighs. She ran her hand over my head as I squeezed her ass. Her eyes closed and her head tilted back.

"I can't compete with a memory, Hanif."

"Why do you want to?"

Her eyes opened and she looked down at me.

"Just… seems like you need to be loved just as much as I do." I stood and towered her.

"I'm eighteen now. What's up?" Grace continued.

"I have a girlfriend."

"Break up with her."

"She understands me. She understands that I can't give the love, attention, and affection y'all need. Not consistently anyway. One day I'll be all up under you, the next I won't want to have anything to do with your ass. Sometimes I might pour my soul out to you and the next minute ignore you like I don't even know you. I'm needy as fuck, but I can be stingy as hell. I promise you, Grace, this ain't what you need."

"But it's what I want."

"I can't."

"You can't or you don't want to?"

"Both."

"Fine."

"Is that it for the questions?"

She nodded and stepped closer to her clothes on the arm of my couch.

"So, you're done?" I asked.

With her hands cupped together in front of her she lowered her head and looked at the ground.

"I'm sorry," I offered.

"Can you just take me home?"

"Why? Because you're in your feelings? If you gon' rock with me you need to learn how to not be so easily effected by the truth, Grace. Get out your feelings and listen to what I'm saying."

"How? How do you expect me to get out my feelings, Hanif? I'm a woman! A Taurus. An introvert. A writer. That's all I am is fucking soul and feelings. So, what do you want me to do? Just turn me off? I can't!"

"I don't want you to go yet."

Her shoulders caved in. Her eyebrows furrowed in confusion.

"The fuck, Hanif?"

I took her face into my hands and kissed her. Finally. She moaned immediately as she wrapped her arms around me. Her mouth opened readily and accepted my tongue. My hands went from her face to her waist and I wrapped her legs around me.

Her body in the middle of my bed looked like something I didn't deserve to see. I understood something at an early age that it takes most people their entire lifetime to figure out, if they ever do – *sex bonds people together*. Oxytocin, the love hormone, bonds people together. Especially in women.

During sex it bonds the woman to her man. During childbirth and breastfeeding it bonds a Mother to her child.

It gives life. It reduces anxiety. It provides a sense of attachment and closeness. It evokes trust. It makes you empathetic. That's why men use sex to make their women forgive them. To get her to stay with him in a dead relationship because she's giving life to it through her sex.

If a woman is mad at you and you make her climax and release that oxytocin, not only will she forgive you but she'll feel closer to you and find herself trusting you even when she probably shouldn't.

Although I couldn't give her what she needed with my words or actions I could give it to her with my body. My mouth. My fingers. My dick. She wasn't ready for the dick yet, but I knew of plenty other ways to satisfy her. Call me selfish, but I just didn't want her to give up on me yet. I know I'd given her a hard time…

"Hanif?" I ignored her as I spread her legs and took in her glistening pussy. "You playing with my emotions."

My mouth covered hers. Her arms wrapped around my neck. My thumb went to her clit as I slid my middle finger inside of her slowly.

I broke our kiss and looked into her eyes.

She was wet as hell.

I watched as her eyes opened and closed. As she licked and bit her lips. As her chest rose and fell. As her legs wrapped around me and fell. As her hips lifted from the bed.

She was wet as hell.

Her wetness felt like ripples cascading my skin.

"Hanif…" Grace moaned as her lips and legs trembled.

Her fingers dug into my arms. She was almost there. Almost fucking there. But her body tensed up. She was fighting it.

"Why you fighting it, Grace?" With a shaking head, her eyes closed as a tear fell from her right eye. A tear falling from the right eye first signaled happiness. She was happy. She was feeling good. She didn't want it to end. "You like that… don't you?"

"Yessss."

"Then cum."

84

With my permission, she allowed her body to submit to my fingers. Her nectar gushed out of her and onto my fingers and I had to pull from all the self-control I had to not plunge my tongue deep inside of her then suck the rest out.

The quaking in her body stopped and I removed my finger. Grace pulled me down to her and kissed me so long and deep her nectar dried on my fingers.

I pulled myself away from her and asked, "How you feel?"

She smiled as I ran my fingers through her hair. That was the exact response I wanted.

"I want more."

"You're not ready."

"I need it."

"That's why you're not ready. You're aching for it. For me. It will... I will consume you, and you won't be able to shake me and let me go."

"But why would I have to let you go?"

"Trust me, baby. Trust my timing."

I was hoping she didn't catch the fact that I'd called her baby, but I knew that she did when she closed and opened her eyes then met mine.

"Just... go take a shower and meet me back here. I'll hold you for a couple of hours before I take you home."

"You gon' cuddle with me, Neef? I don't want to go back home. I wanna stay with you."

Grace sat up in the bed and kissed my lips sweetly. Against my better judgment I pushed her away and agreed. She was the only other woman besides Pria who had been to my home, and she was the first to ever spend the night.

Fuck was I doing?

"Okay, you can stay. Gone take a shower."

She smiled brightly and kissed me quickly before wobbling out of my bed. I sat there for a few seconds before deciding to join her.

Braille

"I don't know which ones I want," I mumbled looking up at Lorenzo.

We both had a fetish for shoes. All of our bags came from Finish Line, Journeys, and Foot Locker. I *did* convince him to come in Hanes with me to get me some sweats and boyshorts. His ass ended up getting more undies and sweats than me! Now we were in H&M and I had about ten pairs of pumps lined up in front of me.

He wouldn't let me pay for anything in the mall. I guess because coming to Nashville for the weekend was his idea. Let him tell it this was his way of thanking me for being there for him and his sisters, but I told him that he didn't have to thank me for that.

His Mother was doing very well with her recovery. Ladia and Chelsea were smart as hell and sweet as pie. And he's my baby. I don't know why he was surprised that I've been by his side. I guess that's just not something he's used to. I guess he's used to doing for others and not having anyone to do for him.

We headed to Nashville right after school. He took his sisters over to their grandma's house and we hit the road. We hadn't even checked into our hotel room before we came to the mall. Lorenzo was excited at first, but now that we'd been here for a couple of hours his face was long and his attitude was live. I couldn't help but smile as I looked up at him.

"Just get all of 'em, B," he said with irritation all in his voice.

That was just it. I really didn't want to spend the money I knew he was making from selling drugs. The only reason why I'd let him buy me things up until this point was because he wouldn't let me buy myself anything.

I didn't work a traditional job, but I made a good amount of money hot pressing t-shirts.

"This is too many. You just pick me a pair."

"Those," he mumbled pointing at the first black pair I tried on. "Those," he mumbled pointing to the nude ones just like it. "Those." He pointed at the red ones. "Those." Then the green ones. "And them gladiator looking sandals like what you got at home. They make your legs look long and sexy."

I looked at the associate that was helping me and she picked up the shoes he'd chosen.

"Now was that so hard? You should've just picked them in the first place, LoLo."

He looked at me then rolled his eyes and I chuckled. A few minutes and a fairly short line later we were leaving the store and the mall. We passed the guest services desk to leave the main entrance and his walking slowed up as he looked inside of a jewelry store.

"You wanna go look for you some more studs?" I asked.

"Nah, I want something for you."

"Lorenzo, I don't even wear jewelry like that. And you've gotten me enough."

"Shut up, B."

Lorenzo grabbed my hand and softly dragged me into the store. We were greeted and he walked over to the rings. I looked up at him skeptically and he smiled.

"Relax, baby. Not yet. I just want to know what size ring you wear for future reference," he assured me.

I nodded and released a breath I didn't even know I'd taken. The entire time I had my ring finger sized he stared at me as if he was in deep thought. I looked at him and smiled. He pecked my lips quickly and softly.

"What kind of ring do you want?"

"Lorenzo..." I blushed and hung my head. "I... I don't know."

"You don't know because you haven't really given it any thought or because that's not something you want with me?"

I couldn't ignore the fear in his eyes. With my hands full of bags I wrapped my arms around him as best as I could.

"I don't know because I've never given it any thought, and I told you I don't wear jewelry like that. All I wear is earrings. Not because that's not something I want with you. I..." I shut my mouth quickly and resisted the urge to tell him that I loved him. It was too soon. *Too soon.* "I can definitely see myself with you for the long haul."

His face softened and he nodded so I released him.

"Cool, well now that I know your size I'll just get you something that I'm sure you'll like."

"If you pick it... I know I'll love it."

He nudged me softly and smiled.

"Let's get out of here before I propose now."

∞

We pulled up at Evins Mill resort, just outside of Nashville, and I looked at Lorenzo skeptically. He was pulling out all the stops. *Was he trying to get some pussy?* He smiled and cut his car off.

"What are we doing here?" I asked unbuckling my seatbelt.

"This is where we're staying."

"Lorenzo…"

"Shhh."

Lorenzo got out of the car and walked over to my side. He opened the door and I got out. I couldn't even say anything to him just yet. What we bought at the mall was in the trunk so we left it there. He grabbed most of our luggage from the backseat. All I had to carry was my makeup bag and purse. I sat down and let him get his grown man on while he checked us in. When he was done he walked over to me with a smile.

"You ready to go check out our penthouse?"

"Penthouse? Lorenzo, we're only going to be here two nights."

"Will you let me spoil you, Braille? Damn."

I stood and kissed his cheek.

"Fine. I'm sorry. Do your thang. Thank you."

Zo lifted my head by my chin and kissed my forehead before leading me to our penthouse. The second I walked inside tears filled my eyes. It was a three-bedroom penthouse, each room having a king bed, private bathroom – with a walk in shower and jetted tub, coffee bar, mini-refrigerator, and a flat screen TV and DVD player. I fell in love with the vaulted hardwood ceilings & screened-in, high-elevation decks with woodsy and waterfall views.

We had a living & dining room area, fireplace, large sitting area and reading room, and a mini beverage station that I couldn't wait to dive into. Lorenzo was putting his IPod on the dock as the tears finally began to fall. He walked over to me with a smile.

"What's wrong? Don't you like it?"

"I love it. It's beautiful. I'm just… a little overwhelmed I guess. Thank you, LoLo."

"Why don't you go take a shower and unwind? Then we can head back to the city for dinner."

I nodded and kissed him. I knew he was against tongue kissing and too much affection but I couldn't resist sliding my tongue into his mouth. He let me for a few seconds then he pushed me away.

"Braille…" he moaned biting down on his lip.

"Okay, okay. I'm done."

I kissed him again and made my way to the bathroom.

Lorenzo

I could never deny it. The closer I got to Braille the more I was sure that she was my rib. The protector of my heart. The discomfort I felt before her was gone. She makes a nigga live and breathe easier now.

I'm sure she probably thought I was up to something... but honestly I just wanted her to myself for a couple of days. My heart was at ease because of her, but my mind was unsettled. It felt like some shit was about to go down and I just needed to get away for a little while for some clarity.

We went to a steakhouse downtown for dinner. Then we went to the pedestrian bridge to walk and talk. There was so much about her that I didn't know... but one thing I knew for sure was that I wanted all of her – good and bad.

I found out that she lived with her single mother. That her mother and father were never together. They just shared one brief moment in time that would forever change their lives. The birth of Braille. Her father was white, and not only was he white but her mother never really wanted him. She said that he reminded her of her ex, and that her father Edward said that her mother Josephine reminded him of his ex. Her sister Camryn's mother, Brenda, who was black too.

So they basically used each other for a night and Braille was what came of their blind love for their exes. Edward is now with Brenda, but Josephine remained single.

She told me that she was going to go to school for nursing. That she wanted to get married and have children after she finished school. We'll see about that. As much as she loved her nephew I'm sure she wouldn't be too mad if I knocked her up before then.

I always knew about her t-shirt hustle, but I didn't realize how successful it was until she pulled up her website. She signed a consignment deal with this nigga named Israel. He had stores all over the U.S. and in each of his stores were a few of her designs.

My baby was doing damn good for herself.

I told her about my post high school plans as well. When I was a young nigga I wanted to be a police officer like my father, but over the years my view of law enforcement had changed. Yea, you have those genuinely good cops that took their vow to serve and protect seriously. But the crooked niggas mess it up for all of them in my eyes.

So I was still going to go to college and get my degree in political science, but I wasn't sure any more about the avenue I wanted to take with it when I graduated. Who knows? Maybe I'll want to be a police officer again. Maybe a lawyer. Maybe a judge. Maybe mayor. Maybe President. The sky ain't even the limit for me. The only thing limiting me is my vision... and my vision is limitless!

"You going to your prom?" B asked me after a moment of silence.

"Nah. I'm going to yours."

She smiled and shook her head.

"How you figure that? You haven't even asked me. Nor do you know what colors I'm wearing."

"I do know what colors you're wearing."

"What colors?"

"I don't know what the hell color it's supposed to be. It's like a reddish purple color." Her mouth opened. I smiled and continued. "The dress itself is sheer nude, but it has red and purple flowers and vines covering a good deal of your skin. Then starting at your waist to the floor it has a sheer reddish purple covering around it. What you call that shit?"

Her mouth was still open as she stared at me. I smiled harder. The back of her hand caressed my cheek.

"How do you know that, LoLo?"

"I asked your sister. I wanted it to be a surprise."

She wrapped her arms around me and kissed my neck.

"Why are you so sweet?"

I shrugged. I really didn't know. I wasn't this type of nigga before her. She pulled parts out of me that were buried so deep I'd forgotten they were there.

"Can we go now? I wanna be in your arms," she whispered into my neck.

That was all I needed to hear.

Braille

Eric Bellinger was playing in the background, but the sound of Lorenzo's pants unzipping drowned his melodious tune out. My eyes had been set on his, but at that sound, my eyes lowered. They traveled down his tatted chest to his boxers. My leg began to shake involuntarily as he slowly pushed them down. I'd felt him numerous times before, but this was the first time I'd seen it. And it was beautiful.

No, like, *really* beautiful. For the most part it was his sandy light shade, but the tip of his head was pink. And as he walked towards me I noticed the bottom of his shaft was slightly darker. He'd stripped me before he stripped himself, so when he put his knees on the bed he pulled me towards the middle of it and spread my legs.

"You sure about this?" Zo asked as his fingers glided across my lips.

"Yes, Lolo."

Lorenzo's face lowered to mine and he slithered his tongue inside of my mouth. They began their slow stroll around each other and my legs wrapped around him immediately. His hands took hold of mine as he bit and sucked my lips, and I felt myself pushing my body up trying to get closer to him.

Our arms went over my head and he kissed me until I was whimpering in desperate need for more. As if he felt me reaching my breaking point, his lips began to move down my body. I felt my juices literally puddling up at his entrance inside of me.

"Mm," he moaned quietly at the sight of it as he bit down on his lip.

I was ashamed of my desire for him. I tried to close my legs, but he grabbed my thighs and kept them open.

"Never hide this from me, B. This is mine. It belongs to me. And I want *every* fucking drop."

His tongue slowly licked between my lips. Pulling up his juices along the way. Zo looked at me with his mouth open, his juice on his tongue, then he closed his mouth and eyes and swallowed it like it was as refreshing as water. His mouth covered my clit and as he sucked I felt my entire body shake just as it did the first time he made me cum.

I moaned and wrapped my legs around his neck. His finger went inside of me and felt around for my G-spot. He hit it and put some pressure on it and made me cum even harder and longer. My hips lifted from the bed and all he did was open his mouth wider to receive me.

My climax was over and I was ready to go to sleep. I'd never felt something so powerful before. With lowered eyes, I grabbed at my hair to try and wake myself up.

"You tapping out?" Lorenzo put the head of his dick at my entrance and I couldn't tell if he was joking or serious. He had that small smile on his face that he normally wore. "If you need a break we can wait, baby. I know this will be your first time."

"I'm ready. Just…"

"I'll be as gentle as I can be, but I can't be too gentle and slow or it'll make me nut."

I nodded, closed my eyes, and inhaled deeply. The feel of him stretching me made me bite down on my lip. With just the tip in he moved in and out of me slowly.

"You okay?" He asked.

My mouth opened and I tried to answer him but I couldn't. I was okay. I was really okay. The smacking noise of my… no *his* juices made him chuckle.

"Your ass okay. You wet as fuck, B."

His tongue began to play with my nipples as he continued to use just his head to dig into my G-spot. I'd learned about it in health, and from the porn I started to watch after he ate me out. But I'd never had anyone to make it feel this good. It got bigger. Like it swelled up. The ridges felt more and more… real and there.

I got hotter. So much wetter. And tighter. Just when I was beginning to trust his ass and let myself go he pushed all of himself inside of me quickly.

"Ahhhh fuck!" I yelled pissed as hell.

He didn't move. He just stayed there. His lips covered mine and he kissed me tenderly. I stroked his back up and down as he finally began to move inside of me. Slowly. Gently. With his full length. Practically pulling himself out of me completely before going in as deep as he could go.

I broke our kiss and moaned. Squeezed his back. His waist. Spread my legs wider. Wrapped my arms around his neck. Took his face into my hands. Tried to look into his eyes, but it felt too good.

"Shit, baby," he moaned into my ear before licking it and biting down on it.

As I learned my body I realized when I felt myself tightening around him I was about to cum. I tapped his back. Trying to get him to stop. But that only made him go faster. It was one thing to cum with him outside of me, but the thought of coming off the dick had me shook.

That was the type of shit that made girls stalk their first love and first sexual partner. I wasn't ready for that.

"That's enough," I pleaded through quivering lips.

He chuckled quietly but stopped when it turned into a moan.

"What you mean that's enough?"

"I'm about to cum."

"Good."

"I don't want to cum."

"Why not?"

He went faster. Then slow. Deep. Then long.

"Lorenzo." I held him closer. Tighter. "Lorenzo. Uhh, LoLooo."

"That's it, baby. Shit, B," he whispered into my lips before kissing me.

"Ohmygoodness," I slurred into his mouth as I felt my body lock up.

My legs unraveled from him and trembled.

"Umhmm," he moaned as his strokes sped up.

As his strokes turned choppy. Less rhythmic and controlled. His mouth opened and his head flung back. Damn. He was coming right along with me.

Lorenzo

Rule called and told me he wanted to rap with me about some shit when I came back from Nashville. On our last day there, B and I went to Nashville Shores as soon as the park opened then we hit the road. After I dropped her off I went to his crib.

He took me down to his man cave and we lit up as usual. Being the oldest of my siblings, and now the man and provider of my household… I had a heavy weight to carry, but these moments that I shared with him always made me feel a little lighter.

"You trust every nigga on your team?" Rule asked me.

I shrugged and took another hit of the blunt.

"Nah. I got a couple niggas that I feel like I can really trust, but that's it."

"How many on your team?"

"Ten."

In just one year I'd set myself up pretty good. My hustle led the way for my niggas like Vega and Canon along with a few other niggas we knew to make a nice little living off this dope shit. The great thing about the position that I was now in was that I never had to touch the product. I was past those days of standing out on the corner.

Now I had niggas doing that for me. All I had to do was buy the shit and give orders out about who gets what and where to sell it. Then I sat back and collected my paper.

"With this new Mayor we got he's cracking down on drug dealers and gang members. He feels like a lot of crime will be solved if they clean up the streets. They aren't concerned with the corner boys like they used to be. They're using the corner boys to get to the head niggas. That's who they want."

"How you find out?"

"You know niggas talk. Since me and Power used to run this shit they still come to us for advice and what not. They just locked Ced up."

"Are you serious? He has niggas on his payroll specifically *for* taking charges!" I almost yelled in disbelief.

"Yea. They're throwing the book at niggas or offering them a free walk for information. There is no in between."

I sat back in my seat and inhaled deeply. My bank accounts were sitting nice. I wasn't ready to stop *just yet*. My mama had a little less than five months to go, and even when she did come out who's to say she was gon' be ready and able to get a job as soon as she got out?

"What you think I should do?"

"When Power and I were in the game we had a small amount of niggas working for us, but they were all niggas we could trust. I had one snake..."

"Marcel. I heard about that shit."

"Right. And he was handled. The reason my niggas were so loyal to me was because I took care of them. I took care of them better than they took care of themselves. Any suspicion was handled immediately. If a nigga crossed us he died. Simple as that. We made it very clear to them that once they joined our family they had only three options – leave and go legit, go to jail if they were caught and trust that we would do all we could to get them out and provide for their families, or die because of their disloyalty."

"And that worked?"

"Hell yea. The first time a nigga got caught in the streets slipping and was knocked his ass tried to snitch. He was dead before he could sign his confession. The second nigga that was knocked kept silent and let our Lawyers work their magic. He was out in three months. The entire time he was gone he had everything he needed while he was locked up and all of his bills were paid by us. When they saw that we weren't playing and that they could trust us they began to get serious about this shit and stop being so damn reckless. After that we didn't have any more problems until Marcel. Make their options clear. They should only have three. And if you can't trust those niggas with your life and freedom they don't need to be around you."

I nodded and released a hard breath.

"Was Braille with you in Nashville?" I nodded. "Y'all serious?" I smiled and nodded. "So that means that you're not only responsible for your life and freedom but hers as well. Can you handle that?"

"Wouldn't be with her if I couldn't."

"Aight. That's my little sister, Zo. I play no games when it comes down to her. You cool, but that's blood. Make sure she straight. Go handle your business. You know what to do."

I nodded and stood. We shook up and he walked me out. He was right, I knew what I had to do. It was time to clean up my team and make sure they knew I refused to take a loss for any nigga.

Jessica

Cam and I haven't been talking as much lately, but I've been talking to Vega since I met him at the mall. To be honest... I'm unsure of what I'm doing. Talking to Vega feels wrong but right at the same time. He asked if he could take me out... well he told me he was taking me out tonight and I agreed. I felt bad as fuck, but I wanted to kick it with him.

There is no doubt in my mind that had Cameron and I just remained friends I wouldn't feel bad at all. We'd still be talking like we always had, but I wouldn't feel tied to him and him alone. I had tons of clothes on my bed but nothing was popping out at me. Probably because I felt so horrible.

Since I was staying at Jabari's house this week I left my room and went into his. I swear I be over my brother's house more than my mama's. The only reason I go back home is because I don't want her to feel like I don't want to stay with her. And to spend time with my niece Christina. I just feel more comfortable and free when I'm at RiRi's house.

I sat on his bed and waited for him to turn around in the chair of his desk and look at me.

"What's wrong?" He asked turning to face me.

"I'm in a bind."

"Regarding?"

"Cam."

"What about him?"

I sighed heavily and started to play with my toes.

"I got back with him, but I met someone else. He wants to take me out tonight."

"What's the problem? If you want to be with someone else just break up with Cam."

"That's just it. I don't want to break up with Cam. I don't think I *want* to be with Vega. I just want to have some fun."

"Vega? The hell kind of name is Vega? Fun? The hell kind of fun? Only fun your young ass better be having is a damn dinner and a movie. Fuck a movie. Y'all don't even need to be sitting in the dark together."

I smiled and held my tongue to give him time to calm down and come out of protector mode.

"I'm just saying I don't want to lose Cam, but I want to... you know... see other people."

"Then why didn't you just stay single?"

I shrugged.

"I don't know. It just happened so fast. He was being his sweet self and I just couldn't help myself."

"Jessica, you're seventeen. You're a senior in high school. You're two months away from being legal. It's okay to want to explore your options and have fun. Just be as open and honest with him as you are with me."

"But I don't want to hurt him."

"Then you will either suffer in silence or hurt him because of your lies. You choose."

"You're right." I stood. "I guess I'll call him now before Vega gets here. And please, RiRi, be nice."

He mumbled something under his breath and returned his attention to his computer. I started to Facetime Cam since that's how we did most of our conversations but I didn't want to see his face. He answered after a couple of rings and my heart literally burned when he said hello.

"Hey, Cam. You busy?"

"Never too busy for you. What's up?"

"Cameron..." I paused and struggled to find my words.

He inhaled deeply into the phone. Like he knew what I wanted to say.

"Say it, Jessie."

"I can't. I don't want to."

Tears immediately welled up in my eyes.

"Say it."

"Cameron... I..."

"Just say it."

"I just... think we... should take a break. Just until you come home for the summer."

"Then what, Jessica? We break up again when I leave for school?" I remained silent. "Swear I'm not about to play with your scary confused inconsistent ass."

"Cameron…"

"No. I don't think you understand how much of me and my life I've given up to make space for you and your inconsiderate ass can't even see or appreciate it."

"That's just it! You shouldn't have to do that for me. For us."

"Why not?"

"We're young. We should be enjoying life."

He laughed and I shook.

"See… that's the problem. We're just… on different levels and I have to respect and accept that. For you… you can't enjoy life loving and being committed to me. But shit, loving you is what gave me life. I get it, Jessie. You're young. You wanna be free. Do you, baby. We're good."

"Cameron, I'm so sorry," I muttered through my sob.

Why did it hurt this fucking bad?

"You don't have to apologize, baby. I love you. Enjoy yourself."

"Will you wait for me?"

"Wait for you?" His voice was on the brink of breaking. I remained silent. Afraid if I repeated myself he'd explode. "What you want me to do, Jessie? Be single while you're out here living it up?"

"No. Of course not. I just… Cameron no other guy has access to my heart. I'm reserving it for you."

"But you want to give other niggas your body?"

"No. That's not… I just… want to be able to go out. Spend time with people. I want someone I can call at ten because I'm bored and go grab something to eat at Waffle House. I want someone I can call after I've had a long day at school and work and we just cuddle.

We agreed that we weren't the type to do long distance relationships, Cameron. That hasn't changed. This shit is too hard! I can't handle not being able to have you when I want you. I'm not saying I want to have sex with other niggas. I'm just saying this is killing me, baby."

"I understand, Jessica. Listen, I um… I sent you a package. It should be arriving tomorrow or the day after. Don't open it. Just return it. I'll put the money in your bank account for the return postage."

"You sent me a package? Cameron…"

"I gotta go. I love you. Enjoy yourself, baby."

"Cam… wait… I'm…"

He disconnected the call. I redialed his number and he let it ring. I redialed his number and he pushed ignore. I redialed his number and his phone was off. *What have I done?*

Vega

I wanted Jessica the minute I saw her, and I ain't give a fuck what her relationship status was. I was *that* young nigga. The one who didn't understand the word no or being told I couldn't have something. Why couldn't I? She was going to be mine just like everything and everyone else I wanted was.

It took me just a few days to convince her to let me take her out. Yea, I knew she had a boyfriend out of state, but I didn't care. He obviously wasn't taking care of his business. If he was I wouldn't have been able to snatch her attention.

I'd been at her door for a few seconds before she opened it. My confident smile fell at the sight of her saddened face and red cheeks, lips, and puffy eyes.

"The hell is wrong with you?" I asked stepping closer to her.

She looked behind her and stepped outside.

"I can't do this, Vega."

"This about your nigga?"

She nodded. Even when she wasn't trying she was fine as hell. Her blonde hair was up in one of them balls at the top of her head. She was wearing a tank top, some Polo basketball shorts, and a pair of Gucci slides. Her face was free of makeup but her red cheeks and full red lips gave her face a pop of color. She had the prettiest slanted doll like eyes I'd ever seen in real life. Then she had the nerve to have a few tattoos on her arms and hand.

"I broke up with him, but I don't feel the way I thought I would feel."

"How do you feel?"

"Like shit."

"Listen, we don't have to go anywhere. Even though I had the most epic date planned." She smiled like I hoped she would. "We can just sit in my car and talk. Is that cool?"

"Yea, that's cool."

We walked to my car and I opened the door for her. When I got inside I cut the air on and the radio down.

"You smoke?" I asked her pulling my blunt from the sun visor.

She nodded and licked her lips. I lit the blunt and took a hit before handing it to her.

"So what happened?" I turned slightly so I could look at her as she talked.

"I don't know. I mean… at first I was cool with the idea of not being with him and him only, but when that shit became reality it hit me hard."

"You love him?"

"As much as I can."

"What you mean as much as you can?"

"It's a long story."

"We got time."

Jessica handed me the blunt and took her shoes off. She pulled her foot up on my seat and leaned back.

"A few years ago my sister was in a very toxic relationship. She ended up getting pregnant and having his baby. I guess she thought having his kid would make him get on some act right but it didn't. He was still lying and cheating and disrespecting her. Abusing her. Then he broke up with her." She laughed softly and shook her head.

"She…" Jessica scratched her eyebrow and looked at me.

I grabbed her hand and rubbed it with my thumb.

"She went into a state that I've never seen before. It wasn't depression. I can't explain it. It was like… she was mad at him, but madder at herself for putting herself in that position. She started sabotaging her own self. Dropped out of college. Starting drinking and smoking heavily. Eventually she overdosed."

"Damn, I'm sorry."

"It's… every day it gets easier. I have B and Grace and two older women that are just like sisters to me. Alayziah and Layyah. So I'm good. But… her baby daddy would come around every once in a while claiming he was checking on their child. On his last visit he raped me. I got pregnant and had to tell Alayziah and my brother."

"He handled that nigga, right? Cause I will."

She smiled but I was dead serious. There were just some things I didn't accept. Abuse to women of any kind was at the top of the list. Right under disrespecting me.

"He did. Permanently." I nodded and squeezed her hand. "I had an abortion and I guess I just shut down. I didn't want to deal with niggas. I didn't want to run into another Chris and I didn't want to turn into my sister because of love and feelings. Then Al and LayLay introduced me to Cam and he changed that."

She smiled again and her eyes watered.

"I let him in and not once has he done anything to make me regret that."

"Then why did you break up with him?"

"I'm not on that love shit right now. It caught me by surprise. I never wanted to like him let alone love him. Then he left for college and left me here with this shit by myself."

Jessica removed her hand from mine and massaged her forehead.

"Then why don't y'all just take a break and pick up where y'all left off when he comes home?"

"That's exactly what I said! But he... he's not that type. He's an all or nothing kind of guy. I just want to enjoy my life. This is my last year of high school. I'm trying to go out, travel, make memories. Not be depressed until the weekend when he comes home."

"That's completely understandable."

She stopped massaging her forehead and looked into my eyes.

"Vega, you don't have to say shit that you think I want to hear to get me. I knew from the moment I saw you whether or not I would give you some play. I knew if I was going to have sex with you. And I knew just where I wanted this to go and what I wanted it to be. So don't lie to me. Don't try to sweet talk me. Always be upfront and honest and communicate with me."

Well, she had my attention and respect.

"I didn't have plans on doing anything but that. I've been nothing but honest with you. I told you from the jump that I wanted you. That ain't changed. I ain't on that love shit either. We can kick it and have fun and do whatever you want to do. We're on the same page, Jessica. I ain't telling you to trust me because I believe in my actions speaking louder than my words, but I will tell you that I'm deserving of that trust."

"Cool. And you'll tell me if you fall in love with me won't you?"

Her smile made me smile.

"And you'll tell me if you decide to get back with your nigga won't you?" She nodded. "Come here. Let me holla at you."

She licked her lips and leaned forward to meet me halfway. I pulled her top lip into my mouth and cupped her neck. I slid my tongue inside and she couldn't even kiss me good for moaning and biting on her lip in desire. I had no idea where we were going to go. How we were going to get there. And how long we would stay. But as of right now... I was willing to accept all that she had to offer.

Grace

Soooo I didn't take Hanif for the *make a girl cum then ignore her for two days* straight type, but that's exactly what he'd done. Since he took me home Saturday morning I hadn't heard from him. He hugged me and gave me a kiss on my nose and told me he'd call me later and that was it. I thought finally he was going to open up and stop being so damn mean and weird but obviously I was wrong.

I let Saturday go by without reaching out to him. Sunday morning, I texted him and when he didn't reply I made up in my mind that I wouldn't reach out to him again. Elle and Camryn stressed to us young girls that we were to command love and respect, not demand it.

When you demand love and respect you are acknowledging the fact that you don't have that within you. You are giving that person power over your emotions and two basic things that should be freely given not earned. When you command it you do so naturally because it's already within you. It's like a magnet is inside of you and because you love and respect yourself and others you attract people who will love and respect you.

Since he wanted to play games and sink back into his hole I decided to increase his demand for me by limiting supply. Camryn said that that was one of the main ways women ended up getting hurt in their relationships. They gave and gave and gave all of themselves to men who didn't deserve them and put in the work to have them then ended up empty because they received nothing in return.

They were teaching us that men don't want anything handed to them easily. Of course they're going to accept you and what you give them, but if you really want to make a lasting impression on him… make yourself unavailable. Don't call him or text him when it's obvious he isn't concerned about making you a priority.

Limit the amount of your time and yourself that you give him. And if he's a real man he'll come for what he wants. It's a part of a man's nature to chase and pursue. Men love to chase. Men should initiate. Women should respond. *If you're making yourself completely open to him and removing his chance to chase you he won't feel any pride in having you.*

And if you aren't your man's pride and prized treasure you won't have his heart. Now that's bible!

I thoroughly enjoyed the workshops Elle had before I left Memphis and now that I was back I was able to go to hers and Camryn's and even talk to them one on one. I was learning so much and in all of my learning I applied it as wisdom and gained strength.

So even though I was slick pissed at Hanif for closing back up I understood that that was just his way. I refused to let it make me feel less than or allow it to get me down. When he wanted me he would come for me. And if I was still available and unattached he could have me.

Even though I knew all of this mentally it didn't stop my heart from aching and forcing me to check my phone yet again as I walked down the hall and made my way to my next class.

"Happy belated birthday."

My eyes closed immediately. My heart dropped. My palms became so sweaty I damn near dropped my phone.

Andy.

"What are you doing here, Andy?" I asked opening my eyes and turning around.

"You didn't think I'd miss your birthday did you? I told you that you wouldn't be able to get rid of me that easily. Did you not believe me?"

"How did you find me?"

"Well, after looking for you all over San Fran I figured you had to have come back home. I went to your parents' house but they didn't even know you were back." My heart dropped even further. "I just took a chance that you came back here for school." My eyes went down to the dead roses in his hands. "I got these for you that day, but you were gone and I couldn't give them to you."

"Andy, you need to go."

"You took my money and left me you heartless ass bitch."

"That was my money! I worked double shifts days on end to save that money. Not you!"

"Did you think about what I was going to do when you left?"

"No, honestly I didn't care. Not after everything you put me through."

"How could you leave me, Grace? I love you. I can't do this shit without you."

"Andy, yes you can. You have family there. You have friends."

"I don't give a fuck about them! I want you!"

His voice was so loud it gained the attention of everyone around us. I took a step back and inhaled deeply.

"Andy, I don't know what's wrong with you... but this isn't normal. And it's not okay. You need to leave."

"I ain't going nowhere without you, Grace. I love you."

I looked into his eyes as tears filled mine. This was *not* the Andy I'd fallen in love with years ago. This wasn't my sweet, gentle, and caring best friend. This was a stranger. A monster I hated to know. His change had been gradual over the years... but this... this was too much.

"How can you call me a bitch and tell me you love me?"

"Because I hate your ass! You don't love me. You don't respect me."

I looked behind Andy at a group of boys standing behind us. One of them I took a class with. He nodded towards Andy and I nodded. They walked over to us and asked if everything was okay.

"I... I need to go," I mumbled as my tears fell.

Not because I was scared, I was, but because I was sad. I had no idea what the hell was going on with Andy, and it broke my heart to see him spiral out of control like this. I tried time and time again to help him. I even suggested that he go to counseling or get some kind of mental tests done to see if something was wrong, but he refused and accused me of being against him.

"We'll make sure you get to class safely," Omar offered.

"No. I need to leave school. Can one of you walk me to my car?"

"I got you," Omar continued.

His arm went around me casually as he turned me and led me out of the school.

"Are you fucking serious, Grace?! You just gon' leave with this nigga in front of me!? This shit ain't over, Grace! I'm not leaving Memphis without you!"

I looked back at him as more tears fell from my eyes. I watched as he fought to get out of the arms that were holding him back. Omar turned my head back around.

"It's cool, Amazing Grace. We got you."

I looked up at him and smiled softly.

"Thanks."

But the truth of the matter was… I didn't trust anyone with me except for Hanif. So as much as I didn't want to go and see him… I had to.

Hanif

When Grace walked into my coffee shop I groaned inwardly. I hadn't called her like I said I would and she looked mad and sad at the same time. It wasn't anything against her. I'd just gotten used to the seclusion I created for myself. I wasn't the type of man to spend all day texting a woman and all of my free time laying up under her.

I'd found out my love language years ago. It was words of affirmation. That's the final piece of why I didn't like talking. All it took was words from a woman to make me fall for her ass. That's how Ciara was able to play me.

Grace seemed like her love language was quality time. She doesn't feel loved and wanted unless a nigga is actually spending time with her. I hadn't completely tossed the idea of being with her out, but it was going to take me some time to break some of my old habits.

By the time she made her way to me I was standing with my hands in my pockets.

"Why you ain't been in pocket?" She questioned.

"I'm sorry?"

"I haven't heard from you since you pulled your finger out of my..."

I grabbed her arm and led her to my office. When I closed the door behind us I sat her in the chair across from my desk.

"Circus acts only attract those who entertain. I'm not about to play with you. If you have something to say use your words and say it. If you miss me and wanted to see me say that. But you gon' get out your feelings and stop playing these games."

"I'm the one playing games?"

She stood and walked up on me. I noticed her eyes were a little puffy like she had been crying. *Had she been crying over me? If she wanted to talk to me that bad why didn't she just call me?* Her hands balled up into a fist, but instead of hitting me she turned quickly and smacked the shit out of me with her hair before trying to walk away.

"Did your crazy ass just slap me?" I asked grabbing her arm again.

Grace looked at me with a smile and tried to remove herself.

"Why haven't I heard for you, Hanif?"

"We're supposed to talk every day?"

Her smile fell.

"Nah. Not at all. I hate I even came up here. Let me go."

"What? Obviously you got something on your mind. Speak." She closed her eyes and shook her head vehemently. "This is exactly why I didn't want to deal with your young ass. You're too emotional."

"I'm not emotional because I'm young you idiot! I'm emotional because I'm attached to your simple ass and you playing with my emotions!"

"I ain't playing with your emotions. I've been nothing but honest with you from the jump, Grace. I've just been to myself. I didn't think anything about it. I told you I wasn't consistent. What do you want from me?"

"I just want you. Are you not even going to try?"

I released her and inhaled a deep breath. Try. Invest. *Was I ready to invest in another woman?*

"Fine. I'm sorry. I'll... call you more. But you know you can call me too, right?"

"I'm not going to be calling you every day, Hanif. If you want to talk to me, you need to put in the effort. Unless you don't want to talk to me. If you don't just tell me and you won't have to worry about me anymore."

My demeanor softened as I pulled her into me. She wrapped her arms around me.

"Of course I want to talk to you. I thought about you a lot."

"Then why didn't you call me?"

"I don't know, Grace. I just... stopped my thoughts."

"So you'd rather go through all of that than to just pick up the phone and call me?"

I nodded.

"Fuck it. I can't. You... I'm done, Hanif. I can't with you."

"Are you serious right now?"

"I'm not used to this. I feel like I'm forcing myself on you and I don't like that at all. I didn't plan on coming here. I didn't plan on seeing you or calling you until you came for me but some shit happened while I was at school and the first person I wanted was you. That's my problem, though, not yours."

She tried to walk away but I grabbed her.

"What happened?"

"Why? You don't care."

"How you figure that?"

"You haven't been caring. Anything could have happened to me and you wouldn't know because your difficult ass can't pick up the damn phone!"

"So let me get this straight… you came because you wanted to talk to me… but you don't want to talk to me?"

Grace nodded and crossed her arms over her chest so I continued…

"I'm sorry, baby. I'm not apologizing again. I told you I wasn't consistent. You can accept that and my apology and we can move forward or you can leave."

Her nose crinkled and I smiled and tried to conceal it by licking my lips.

"I accept your apology, but I can't accept your actions. I… need more and I don't want to feel like I'm changing you or settling."

"So what you saying?"

Grace stepped closer to me. Stood on her tip toes. And placed a soft kiss on the side of my lips. Her head lowered and I knew she was fighting back tears. She pulled the key to the car I'd given her from her key ring.

Grace opened my hand and put the key inside. For a second she kept her hand in mine.

"Goodbye, Hanif. I can't keep waiting for you."

I nodded my understanding.

"How are you going to get home, Grace?"

"My best friend followed me here in her car."

"So you planned on ending this all along?"

"We don't have anything to end, Hanif! What do we have?"

"More than I've had with anyone in a long time. I know I ain't the easiest nigga to get along with… but I swear I'm worth it."

"I know you are… but I have too much going on to have to worry about you too."

"What happened? Talk to me." She shook her head as her tears finally began to fall. I sat on the edge of my desk and pulled her into me. "Who followed you here?"

I went into her pocket and grabbed her phone.

"Braille."

After pulling Braille's name up on her phone I dialed her number.

"Lawd have mercy. You dan gave in already?" Braille asked as soon as she answered the phone.

I smiled. "Nah. She ain't gave in yet. She giving me a hard time. You can go on home. She won't be needing a ride."

After a moment of silence, she asked, "You sure?"

"Yep. She's good."

"Aight. Be careful with my sister, Hanif."

"No doubt."

I ended the call and put her phone on my desk.

"You hungry or thirsty?" She shook her head no. "What happened, Grace?"

"He was there."

"Who?"

"The reason I came back to Memphis."

"Okay, I need more than that to understand what's going on."

She sat in front of me.

"I left Memphis when I was sixteen. My father he's... very distant. He doesn't believe in saying he loves you. Likes you. Really he doesn't talk much at all. He never showed me any kind of attention and affection. He always said the way he showed his love was by providing for me and my mama and protecting us."

Damn. That's why she was drawn to me. Because I was doing practically the same thing her father was doing.

"My mama... I don't know why she accepted his shit but she stayed with him and told me that there was nothing we could do to change him. We just had to accept him as he was. When I was thirteen Andy and his parents moved next door to us. We hit it off fast.

At first it was platonic. He was my best friend. He listened to me. He talked to me. He saw me. He acknowledged me. He... made me feel like I existed and mattered."

She stopped talking as she went deep into her thoughts.

"Grace..."

"Yea. Sorry. We were friends for three years before he decided to go to California for college. Looking back at his desire for me to go with him then... it was the first sign that he was changing. I couldn't see it then because I was on the inside looking out. He was way too attached to me. He didn't want to be without me. He felt like he couldn't do what he was trying to do without me.

So we moved to San Francisco and at first it was cool. But his moods started changing quicker and quicker. He started cheating and... I had sex with him because I thought that would get him to stop but it didn't. That just made it harder for me to leave.

He would force me to have sex with him. It was just a lot of shit going on. I was trying to go to school and work to pay our bills because he sucked at maintaining his responsibilities. The final straw was when I found out that we were four months behind on our rent. I thought he was paying but he was using the money on unnecessary shit and trips.

I worked hard. Stacked my money. And the day before I planned on paying off our balance one of his friends stole the money. I was pissed. I confronted him and told him I was ready to go home. He didn't want me to leave of course and he told me that he wouldn't let me leave him but I didn't take his threat seriously. Andy got the money back, but instead of paying the rent I sold my Camaro and pocketed all the money and came home.

He had been blowing my phone up so I called and got my number changed on my way here. I thought he was going to let me go but he was at my school today."

"Did he touch you?"

"No. He was just very... disrespectful. He wasn't himself. He was all over the place emotionally. One minute he was telling me that he loved me and couldn't do this without me and the next he was telling me that he hated me and was calling me a bitch. I don't know if he has something going on mentally or if he's on something or what. But that wasn't Andy. That wasn't Andy."

"You want me to protect you?"

"No, Hanif. I don't want you to do anything for me. I just... had a long and bad day and for some reason I allowed myself to get used to you making my long and bad days better and easier."

"I still can. If you let me."

She shook her head and lowered it.

"That will only make this harder. I don't need you to be my protector."

"Then what do you need me to be?"

"You can't see it?"

I took her face into my hands and looked into her glossy eyes.

"I see a young broken girl who attracted me into her life because of the parts of me that are like her father." Her eyes closed as tears fell from them. "I'm sorry, Grace. I wish I could give you what you need…"

Her fingers covered my lips. Her eyes found mine.

"I'd be better off with Andy."

She stood and kissed my forehead.

"Just… let me protect you, Grace."

"I'll be fine." She sniffed and walked behind the chair she was seated in. "May I have my phone? I need to call B. But knowing her she's probably still outside."

"You need a car, Grace."

"I can pay to have mine fixed."

"That car is a piece of shit." She smiled surprisingly. "Take the car, Grace."

Grace looked into my eyes and what little pieces of my heart remained shattered even more.

"Thanks," she mumbled.

I handed her her phone, but I didn't release my hold on it.

"Let me protect you."

"I'll be fine. I can handle him."

"Obviously you can't."

"Neef…"

"Let me protect you and take care of this nigga for you. I need to do this for you, Grace."

"Why?"

"I can't explain it. I just would feel like less of a man if I didn't help you."

"Fine. What are you going to do?"

"Don't worry about that. Just give me his information and his parent's information." I stood and grabbed a pen and a piece of paper. "Write down anywhere in Memphis you think he could be staying. If I can't find him, I'll just be at your school tomorrow. If he found you and wants you he'll be back."

When she was finished writing she handed me the piece of paper.

"Did he see what car you were driving?"

"Nah. He shouldn't know where I live either."

"Good. So the only time he'll be an issue is when you're at school?"

She nodded.

"Why don't you just stay with me? Just to be on the safe side."

"Hanif…"

"Fine. Why don't you just stay with me because I want you to?"

"Hanif, you're confusing the hell out of me."

I smiled and walked over to her.

"This is what you wanted. Me. This is me. You still want me… don't you?"

"No."

"You don't?"

She shook her head no. I nodded and unbuttoned her jeans.

"Neef…" My hand went into her panties and it was drenched with her wetness. "Fine. Yes, I want you, but I can't do this to myself. I just got out of one crazy relationship. I'm not trying to be with a man that has just as many issues as Andy."

I removed my hand and took a step back. She was dead set on leaving.

"If you want to help me out with him that's fine and I appreciate that… but that has to be it."

The funniest feeling overtook me. All of this time I've been trying to avoid getting close to her because I didn't want to lose her, but now that I had… it hurt just the same.

"Okay. I'll take care of it."

She nodded and took a step back. I handed her the key. Grace looked at it briefly before taking it.

"I'll call you when it's handled," I continued.

"Thanks."

I moved to the side so she could leave. There was nothing I could do but let her go. She had every right to refuse to settle for me and this current state I was in. It wasn't fair of me to keep her on the tips of my fingers just because that was what was convenient for me.

She thought I'd been reserving my heart for my ex, but it seemed as if I'd been guarding it to make sure no one else had access to it until her.

Now I just needed to remember how to open it.

Grace

Hanif called me around midnight. Had I been asleep I wouldn't have answered but B, Ms. Josephine, and I had been up late watching movies so I hadn't settled in yet. He told me that he was outside and I shot up from the couch to go and see him.

Showing no concern for my appearance, my hair remained in the two French braids I had it in. I kept on my boxers and tank top too. I did put on some earrings, though.

When I walked outside he was leaning against his car with the most nonchalant look on his face, which calmed my nerves.

After we got in the car he mumbled, "It's handled."

"Already?"

"I wasn't nicknamed Savage for nothing, Grace."

"What did you do? He's not dead is he?"

"No. Thanks to his parents."

"What happened, Hanif?"

"I went to his parents' home. He was there. I beat his ass. I was about to drag him out the house and take him with me to finish him off but his mother begged me not to. Did he tell you the reason he had to go to Cali was because his parents didn't consider art a real career?"

"Yea… how do you know?"

"Grace… he's… suffering from borderline personality disorder."

Borderline personality disorder?

"What?"

"Do you know what that is?"

"Yea… I just… can't believe it."

"His mother said he left because they were trying to get him to stay here for treatment under their care. He's overly sensitive and easily provoked. He took that as them rejecting him."

"That would explain how he could switch up on me like that. I *knew* something was wrong. So what are they going to do?"

"There's really nothing they can do. He's an adult in the eyes of the law so they can't force the medicine on him. He has to choose to take it himself. They did say that they were going to try and convince him to start it before he left, though."

"And if he doesn't?" He stared at me in silence. "Maybe I could get him to take it."

"How, Grace?"

"I don't know." My eyes watered. "He was there for me. I just… feel like I need to be here for him."

"If you want to talk to him I'll take you to see him when he wakes up…"

"Wakes up?"

"Yea. He was unconscious when I left. As I was saying, I'll take you to see him, but I don't want you talking to him by yourself."

"That'll work."

"Can I take you out?"

I looked over at him in confusion. His quick change of topic threw me off. And I could have sworn when I left from seeing him earlier that we weren't going to try and take it there anymore.

"Take me out?"

"Yea… you know… on a date."

"Hanif, I'm not about to play with you. All this not communicating shit…"

"I won't do that to you. I know that's something you need to feel loved. I won't deny you of that."

As much as I didn't want to… I smiled.

"Fine."

"When?"

"Um, let's see… tomorrow I have to go and get fitted for my dress. I have less than a month to…"

"What dress?"

"My prom dress."

"Can I take you to that too?" I looked at him skeptically and scratched my neck. "I didn't get to go to mine. I think it would be nice to take you to yours."

"Hanif, don't commit yourself to something you're not going to be able to follow through on."

Hanif grabbed one of my braids and pulled my face to his. He kissed me and I practically melted against him. He might not be the best with words, but he damn sure knew how to work his fingers and tongue.

And that I just couldn't understand. How could a rapper and poet not be able to express himself? He could. His stubborn ass just chose not to.

"If I say I'm going to do it I'm going to do it, Grace."

"You said you were going to call me and you ain't do that."

He smiled and shook his head.

"Let that shit *go*, girl."

"Hanif?"

"Yes, baby?"

"Pria."

"I ended it."

"Hanif?"

"Yes, baby?"

"Can you... make me... feel like that again?"

"Get in the backseat."

I almost squealed as I crawled into the back. He opened his door and got in the backseat the correct way. I was about to pull my boxers down but his hand around my wrist stopped me.

"I'm about to make you cum without touching you."

"How?"

"By talking to you, and showing you that you can trust me to lead you."

"That is not going to work."

"You don't think so?"

"Nope."

He smiled and nodded.

"For women who are in tune with their feminine energy they have to feel safe and relaxed to cum. A woman submitting herself to a man and allowing him entrance inside of her is one of the biggest ways that she shows that she trusts him. You might think that your pussy is where you experience the most sexual pleasure, but it's actually your brain."

His hand went to my chest and he pushed me back into the seat before removing it.

"I want you to relax, Grace. Inhale and exhale deeply. Relax your body and your mind. Breathe deeply. Slowly."

I released all of my thoughts... besides the ringing *does this nigga think this is going to work*... and inhaled and exhaled deeply.

"Picture yourself in the ocean. Allow those waves to rock you back and forth. As you inhale and exhale slow and deeply feel the waves underneath your body. Open your mouth and breathe through it instead of your nose."

I did as I was told. My heart felt wider. My stomach felt empty. My pussy felt open. Wet. I felt myself rocking back and forth without my damn permission.

"Spread your legs wider."

I did as I was told. As I inhaled I felt my breath in front of my body. With my exhale it felt like my breath traveled down my spine.

"Increase the speed of your breathing."

I did as I was told. I heard myself moaning as I inhaled.

"Faster."

"Mmmm…"

My breathing picked up. My rocking sped up.

"At the same time I want you to take a deep breath in and hold it, then squeeze that pussy tight. Do it now."

I did as I was told. When I thought I was about to run out of breath he whispered…

"Breathe, Grace."

I exhaled and my pussy throbbed. My legs shook. The top of my body convulsed. I damn near fell forward as I moaned but he grabbed me and held me until my orgasm subsided. When my breathing returned to normal I opened my eyes and looked at him.

What the hell had I just experienced?

Hanif ran his fingers down my neck and I shivered under his touch.

"How you feel?" He asked softly.

"Good. That was… how did you do that?"

He chuckled and pulled me into his chest.

"That wasn't me. That was all you."

"That was intense. I'm wet as hell. I'm probably gon' have a wet spot when I go in the house."

He laughed even harder but I was serious.

"Grace?"

"Yes?"

"I really *do* like you."

I looked up at him and smiled. Now he was the one being serious.

"You do?"

"I do. I'm committed to showing you too."

I nodded and bit down on my lip.

"K," I said softly.

His hand went down my hair a couple of times before he leaned down and kissed me. I don't know how long we sat out there, but when the sky started lighting up I went back inside and fell face first into my bed.

Hanif

The first place I took Grace on our date was to The Dixon Art Gallery and Gardens. We walked around different galleries and gardens and got to know each other. I learned some new things about her. She planned on going to school for Creative Writing. She enjoyed writing of all kinds, but she wants to write screenplays and books.

She's the only child, but her two best friends are like her sisters. Along with two older women named Elle and Camryn. She seems crazy about them and happy to have them in her life.

She holds a lot in and takes and takes and takes then breaks down completely. She gives her all and is offended and hurt quickly because of how much she pours into others.

Grace was a beautiful soul that needed to be protected, and I planned on doing just that.

We had dinner at a restaurant called The Beauty Shop. I drove all the way back to her crib just for her to tell me she wasn't ready to go home yet, so I took her back to my spot. I gave her my t-shirt as I did the first time she came over and went to change myself.

When I returned she was looking at the pictures I had over my fireplace of my family and I. I wrapped my arms around her waist and kissed her neck. She turned to face me and looked at me like there was something she wanted to say but couldn't.

Then she smiled and said...

"I exist in the depths of solitude. Pondering my true goal. Trying to find peace of mind and still preserve my soul. Constantly yearning to be accepted and from all receive respect. Never compromising but sometimes risky and that is my only regret.
A young heart with an old soul.
How can there be peace? How can I be in the depths of solitude when there are two inside of me? This duo within me causes the perfect opportunity to learn and live twice as fast as those who accept simplicity."

I smiled. That was one of my favorite poems.

"That's... Grace..."

"Every time I read that poem I think about you."

"You know what poem makes me think about you?"

"What?"

"In your chaos I was your peace. In your stress I was your relief. But can you tell me how happy you'll be when you realize the problems you'll have with me? I'm so fucking needy. I need to be touched, kissed, and hugged. I need your time. I'm a little insecure and I need to be assured that you're mine.

I'm really stubborn. I don't like to be told what to do. And I can be extremely inconsistent about how I feel about you. It doesn't take much to irritate me and I shut down when I don't get my way. Sometimes I'll need to be near you desperately then I'll ignore you for days.

I act like I don't care sometimes because I over care and I'm afraid you'll under understand why without you I remember I'm lonely. I'm sure you weren't expecting all of this when you wished you had me. Well you have me. Do you feel like I tricked you?

Because I tried to hide these things before you let me get you. I was so focused on bringing you peace I didn't want to add to your stress. But every day that I have you, you add to my mental and emotional wealth.

In being there for you I realized... you're the peace to the chaos that is me. You're the peace to the chaos that was me. Your beauty has turned me into a beautiful disaster. And I can't wait to see what happens in our next chapter."

She smiled and hung her head as she normally did when she was fighting back her tears.

"Who wrote that?"

"Me."

Her eyes returned to mine.

"For... me?"

My fingers went into her hair and massaged her scalp. I kissed the side of her eye and confirmed.

"For you." Her hands gripped my waist and she squeezed as she looked into my eyes. "I probably need to get you home, Grace."

"I don't want to go. I wanna stay with you."

"Is that what you're going to do every time you come over?"

She nodded and hugged me and I smiled.

"You don't want me to stay, Neef?"

"I want you to stay."

"But?"

"But I don't know if I'll be able to practice the self-control I used the first night you were here."

"That's fine."

I chuckled and pulled her off of me.

"It's not time for that yet. Sex will just make this even more difficult and you even more attached. I don't want to make this harder for you. I'm trying to make it easier."

The pout on her face make my dick hard. *As hell.*

"Fine, Hanif."

"Did you enjoy yourself tonight?"

She nodded and removed herself from my chest.

"Yes. We might as well go watch Alvin and the Chipmunks since you ain't giving up the dick."

Grace headed for my bedroom and it took me a second to respond and walk behind her.

"Grace, I am not watching that shit."

"It's funny."

"Ion care. I'm not watching that."

"But Hanif, I'm the guest. I should get to choose."

"Man, your ass stopped being a guest the second you stayed overnight. You damn near stay here now."

"Well, we can watch The Color Purple."

"We watched that long ass movie last time you were here!"

"It's my favorite."

"It's my house."

"Neef!"

Braille

Me: What you wanna do tonight after prom? Jessie said Vega wants to do an after party.

Zaddy: Each and every part of you.

Me: Lorenzo, stop being a perv. I could use some Facetime right now though.

Zaddy: Bring that pussy to me and I'll give you all the Facetime you need.

Me: I can't. We're at the spa now. When we leave here we're going to get our nails and hair done.

Zaddy: So I can't see you until I pick you up tonight is what you saying?

Me: Basically, that's why I asked you what you wanted to do after prom.

Zaddy: I told you what I wanted to do. Every part of you.

"You must be texting Lorenzo," Grace said grabbing my attention.

"Why you say that?"

"Cause you keep giggling and squeezing your legs together," Jessie added.

I rolled my eyes and shook my head.

"So?"

"Y'all are cute. I'm happy you're so happy with him," Grace continued.

I let out a small pleasurable sigh at the thought of my baby. We've gotten closer than I thought was possible this quickly. We're together almost every day, and if we're not together we talk in the morning before we start our day and at night before we end it.

Tonight would be the first time he met my parents and I'm so excited and nervous! There's something important that I need to talk to him about, and I'm not really sure how he's going to feel when I do. Just when I think I have him figured out he says or does something that shows me that there's so much about him that I still have to learn.

Looking over at my girls my heart felt so light. Jessica... I've never known a girl like Jessica. Well, Cam tells me that she was like Jessica before she met Rule. It's like... she just can't fully give herself to a man. She genuinely doesn't want love. Now I know that we're still young, but what young girl doesn't want love and marriage? The fairytale wedding and happily ever after? Shit, I was dreaming about that when I was seven!

She doesn't really talk about Cameron much. There's a box that he sent her on the edge of her dresser at her brother's house. Every time I go over I'm tempted to open it and see what's inside, but I resist and wait for her to open up to me about it.

Vega is good for her. He's giving her the fun that she craves. Vega is Lorenzo's best friend and right hand man in his street business, so he's sitting on pretty money just like Zo is. So, every weekend since they've met Vega has been taking her out. Sometimes to places here in Memphis. Sometimes out of town. Happy looks good on her. If this is what she wants and needs and she's satisfied... I'm cool with that!

Grace is finally returning to the sweet crazy lovable Grace she was before she got tangled up with Andy. She told me that she went to see him right after his run in with Hanif and he promised her that he would take his medicine regularly. I guess that was something you had to see to believe. As long as he didn't come at my girl again I was cool. But with Hanif hanging around I honestly didn't see Andy or anyone else as a threat to her. He took care of her.

And my LoLo takes care of me.

Lorenzo

When I pulled up to Braille's crib I sighed. Her driveway was full of cars. I wanted to get in and get out so I could get in her, but it looked like her whole damn family was here to see us off. I got out and went up to the house and the first person I saw was Rule.

"Her pops is here so be aware of the way you look at her," Rule warned me as we walked inside.

"She look that good?" My dick was getting hard already.

"My little sis is beautiful. That's all I'll say. Edward is a cool laid back nigga... well white dude, so be respectful."

I smiled and ran my hand over my hair. I didn't care. I was just ready to see my baby. He introduced me to her parents and Camryn's mother Brenda was there as well. I scooped her nephew Reign up in my arms and sat down, but the second I did Camryn came in the living room with glossy eyes. I stood and handed Reign to Rule.

"Is she... she ready?" I asked Camryn.

She nodded and smiled softly.

"Lorenzo... you better take care of my sister," she mumbled before kissing my cheek.

"I got her, Cam."

And I meant that... but my emotions were conflicted. This morning, two of my corner boys were picked up. They were arrested on felony charges so I couldn't bail them out. I couldn't even visit them. After my talk with Rule, I held a meeting and told them what to do in case they were ever arrested so I was hoping they stuck to that shit, but with niggas these days... you never can tell.

I scheduled an emergency meeting for in the morning and I shut my operation down for tonight. As heavy on my mind as that shit was I tried not to let it faze me. B could always tell when things weren't right with me and I didn't want to ruin tonight for her. I wanted it to be something she'd remember for the rest of her life.

As heavy on my mind as that shit was... when I saw her... it all faded away.

Her hair was in a long ass ponytail that went down to her ass – giving me the perfect view of her gorgeous face. Her makeup was natural and light. The only bold thing was her lipstick that was the same color as her dress.

Both sides of her nose was pierced so she had a stud in her left nostril and a hoop in her right. But I couldn't stop staring at those eyes. Those gray eyes. Those eyes hypnotized me. My eyes kept traveling from the sheer sash around her waist to her face.

I don't know how long I stared at her but she covered her face and Rule nudged me in my back.

"Dude, give her the corsage," he instructed.

I nodded but my feet still wouldn't move. *God, she was beautiful.* Braille smiled and slowly walked over to me. She looked at me briefly before putting my boutonnière on me.

"Baby… you look amazing," I mumbled into her forehead.

B looked up at me and smiled.

"Thank you. You look quite handsome yourself."

My arm wrapped around her and I pulled her closer to me.

"LoLo," she whispered.

I remembered that we weren't alone and put some space between us. Inhaling deeply, I slid the corsage on her wrist, took her hand into mine, and brought it to my lips. She blushed and hung her head.

"You ready to go?" I asked, but really it was a plea. All I needed was one picture at the prom, one dance, and then to have her in the middle of my bed.

"No, you can't leave yet! We have to get some pictures of you two together. Here… turn around and wrap your arms around her," her mother instructed.

"Gladly," I muttered pulling Braille close.

She looked up at me and smiled as she shook her head. I shrugged. Shit, I was ready to get this over with. B felt my dick against her because she looked at me again and her smile widened. I smiled and squeezed her.

"Okay, three pictures and that's it," Braille said looking from her mother to Camryn.

"Man, forget all that. We taking pictures until I run out of storage on my phone," Camryn replied walking over to Ms. Josephine.

I groaned and looked over at Rule for help, but he had his phone out too. This was about to take all night.

Jessica

I hadn't heard from Cameron since I broke up with him about a month ago. The package arrived the next day as he said it would, but I didn't send it back. I opened it. It had about twenty handwritten letters in it. On each envelope in permanent marker he had small notes on when I should read them.

The first one had written – FOR WHEN YOU MISS ME. The second one had written – FOR WHEN YOU'RE MAD THAT YOU CAN'T HAVE ME. The third one had written – FOR WHEN YOU'RE HORNY. The fourth one had written – FOR WHEN YOU'RE HAPPY AND I CAN'T ANSWER MY PHONE TO SHARE IT WITH YOU. And so on and so forth all written boldly in capital letters.

Over the past month I'd opened and read them all. Feeling just a little closer to him. And each time I opened one I wrote him back and mailed them to him. He had to be getting them because they were never returned, but he still didn't call or text me. He still didn't answer my calls or text messages. Eventually I gave up and stopped trying to reach out to him. I still wrote him the letters, but I stopped calling and texting. And emailing. And Facetiming.

I'd been spending a lot of time with Vega. He's like... the complete opposite of Cameron. Cameron is a good guy. He's the one you bring home to daddy, in my case my brother, and marry. Vega is the nigga you have fun with and enjoy life with until you're ready to settle down. He's the bad boy that you want to tame, but at the same time really don't worry about because he is who and how he is and it's so refreshing.

After not hearing from Cam I agreed when Vega asked to take me to my prom. I think he really asked because Lorenzo wasn't going to their prom and he didn't want to go without his best friend. So, since Zo was taking B to our school prom his ass asked me to mine. Whatever his reasoning I agreed and I was glad to be hanging on his arm... until Jabari came to my door and told me that Cameron was in the living room.

Cameron was in the living room?

What the hell for?

I hadn't heard from him in forever and he randomly shows up the night of my prom? I couldn't even go out as soon as he told me. I just looked at myself in the mirror and tried to drown out the laughing and talking coming from the front room. Not only was Cameron there, but my sisters Alayziah and Layyah were there with their husbands and their best friends Kailani and Imani as well. Their husbands were there too. So, basically I had a house full that were about to possibly witness all hell breaking loose depending on how civil Vega would act when he arrived.

Vega.

I needed to get Cameron out of there before Vega arrived. After inhaling a deep breath, I walked out of my bedroom and towards the sound of laughter and happiness. Alayziah was the first person to notice me. She jumped up immediately and ran towards me. Pulled me into her arms. And kissed my neck because she didn't want to mess up the makeup on my face.

The whole time she did my eyes were on Cam and his on me. He stood and walked over to me. I took a step back and looked away from him to avoid getting pissed off.

"What are you doing here, Cam?"

"I thought you said I could take you to your prom?"

"Yea... but I haven't heard from you in a month."

"I mean... I... couldn't. But... I wanted to keep my commitment to you even though you broke yours to me."

I let out a stressed breath and took a step back.

"You should have told me you were coming, Cameron." The doorbell rang. "I... made... other..."

"Shit," Layyah mumbled.

I didn't have to look back. I smelled Vega's cologne.

"Arrangements," I finished.

Vega's arm wrapped around me from behind and he kissed my cheek. I looked at him, but his eyes were focused on Cameron.

"I'm sorry," I mumbled removing myself from Vega's grip. "I didn't know you wanted to still take me."

Cameron's fingers slid down my cheek. My eyes closed and I prayed my tears back.

"Aye, my guy, keep your hands to yourself," Vega ordered as he removed Cameron's hand from my face.

I looked at RiRi for help. He stepped towards us and I looked back at Vega with pleading eyes. He looked down at me briefly before returning his attention to Cameron. Cameron was a good guy, but if he was anything like his brother Israel he was a hot head too.

"I am. She *is* me." Cameron grabbed my arm and pulled me closer to him.

Vega grabbed my other arm and pulled me to him.

"Alright, both of y'all need to let her go. Jessie, you need to choose which one of these niggas you want to go with," Jabari demanded pulling both of their hands from me.

I looked from one to the other with tears filling my eyes.

"You know what? You don't have to choose, Jessie. I don't even know why I came here thinking we could work this out. You want him? You can be with him."

Cameron walked away and I reached my arm out to stop him, but the words wouldn't come out of my mouth. Israel stood and walked out behind him. Then Layyah stood and walked over to me.

"Don't let this shit get you down, baby girl. He'll be fine. Go out and enjoy yourself." She hugged me and left.

I flicked my tear away before it could fall from my eye.

"Well... I... guess... we should take the pictures so you guys can get out of here," Alayziah said.

I looked at her and she hung her head to avoid my saddened eyes. I wanted no pictures. This was one night I wanted to quickly forget.

Vega

I take, but no one can take what's mine.

I started to question Jessica about that nigga being there, but since she was with me I didn't see the need to. She was pretty as hell tonight and I felt bad for almost ruining it.

The dress she had on wasn't really a dress. It was a two-piece crop top and skirt set. It was cream with flowers at the bottom of it. The sleeveless design showed off her tats and made her look classy but sexy at the same time.

Her hair was in those big loose wavy curls. The makeup she had on made her face look like it was glowing. Her lipstick wasn't wet like regular lipstick. I think she called it matte, but it made her lips look even fuller. I'd been nibbling on them junts all night. Surprisingly she let me.

I thought she would have been in a fucked up mood because of her ex, but I told her if that's what she wanted and where she wanted to be she could get from 'round me. I wasn't for that depressing in your feelings shit. Life was too short to not have what you wanted and be happy while you had it.

By the time we made it to the prom she'd loosened up and seemed to be herself. We stayed for about an hour before I asked her if she was ready to head out. She wasn't dancing with me or her friends. She was just hugged up on me with her hair in my chest and her feet on the seat next to her.

In a chill ass mood.

Swear I couldn't get enough of this girl. It's like... she didn't let nothing keep her down for too long.

When we left I asked her where she wanted to go. I had already rented a condo downtown on the river for the night, but if she wanted to go out to eat or back home or some shit I was cool with that too. We hadn't had sex yet, but it was literally just a matter of time because we got tested together and I hadn't fucked around with nobody else since I started talking to her.

Jess said she wanted to spend the night with me so I took her to the condo. The first thing she did was get out of her dress and into some basketball shorts and a tank top. Her hair went up into a ball and she removed the makeup from her face.

And at that moment… she was the most beautiful that I'd ever seen her.

I stepped out to take a call from Zo. He told me that he wanted to have a meeting in the morning and wanted me there. I agreed, but I was more than likely going to be late. This would be my first time spending the night with Jess and I wanted to take advantage of every second of it.

When I returned to the condo she was out on the balcony leaning against the railing. Looking into the distance at the river. My chest went to her back and she wrapped my arms around her.

"You good, Jess?"

"I'm good. Thanks, Vega."

"So what you wanna do?" Her body turned and she faced me. "I mean… it's chill as hell on the river. You wanna go for a walk? Get something to eat? Netflix? Sleep?"

She smiled and ran her hands down my chest.

"What you wanna do?"

"You."

Her smile widened until she licked her lips.

"We can do that."

I smiled and took her face into my hands. My plan was to kiss her but my head tilted as I looked into her eyes. Her beautiful eyes. Something happened. In my heart. It skipped a beat. The longer she looked at me the weirder I felt. I didn't like this feeling, but I couldn't turn away. She'd captivated me.

"What's wrong?" Jess asked as her arms wrapped around me.

"Nothing," I lied.

"You sure?"

I remained quiet as I nodded and grabbed her hand to lead her back into the condo. We made it to the bedroom but I was in no rush to get her in the bed. *The fuck was going on with me?* She looked up at me with those eyes… those eyes… damn her and those eyes. *Was I catching feelings?* No. Couldn't be. Not me. We agreed. There would be none of that.

"Vega..."

I kissed my name from her lips. Her mouth opened and made room for my tongue. I sucked hers and she moaned then bit down on my bottom lip. Pulling away, I stared at her for a few seconds.

"Vega? What is it?"

"I like you," I admitted softly.

She chuckled and hugged me.

"Okay? I like you too. Is that a bad thing?"

"I didn't *want* to like you."

"Why not? What did you want to do?"

Her chin rested on my chest and she looked up at me. *Why did she have to look up at me?*

"I just wanted to kick it with you and shit. You know I'm leaving for Dallas after we graduate."

"You're starting to get attached to me?"

I nodded and kissed her forehead.

"That's understandable. We've been kicking it tough for a month straight."

"But we promised..."

"Don't overthink it. I like you. You like me. Let's just enjoy each other while we can."

"I don't want to be another Cameron in your life."

Damn. *Did I just say that shit? Out loud?*

"What you mean?"

"Nothing. Forget it."

"No... what do you mean?"

"I ain't tryna be out here lovesick over your ass while you on to the next."

She looked towards the ceiling, licked her lips, and took a step back.

"So what you wanna do, Vega? You wanna end this shit now? I thought we were on the same page?"

"We were. I guess I'm ready to go to the next. Which is why I think we need to just... chill out on this."

"Fine."

"Fine?" Jess shrugged and took another step back. "That's all you have to say?"

"What you want me to say? I don't want to be in a relationship. That hasn't changed. I really like you and I enjoy spending time with you, but I'm not trying to go through what I went through with Cam all over again. It would be cool if you weren't going to Dallas, but that would just be like déjà vu all over again."

"You disappointed in me? I dan fucked around and caught feelings for your ass."

She smiled and wrapped her arms around my neck.

"I'm not disappointed. I am... kind of. I really do like you, and I am going to miss you, but I'm glad you told me before we had sex."

I squeezed her ass and pulled her deeper into me.

"We still can."

"No. That will make you leaving harder. You can eat the pussy, though."

"Man... what you gone give me in return?"

"Nigga... nothing!"

I mushed her cocky, silly ass away from me but pulled her closer at the same time. My lips went to hers. This time when I kissed her I felt more at ease. This time she was the one that pulled away.

I pulled her shirt over her head slowly to give her time to stop me... but she didn't. Sitting on the edge of the bed I pushed her shorts down slowly while looking up at her to give her time to stop me... but she didn't.

My lips placed light kisses on her stomach as I pulled her panties down. She gripped my shoulders and squeezed gently. I dipped my tongue into her belly button and she tried to remove herself from my grip but I kept her there.

After placing her leg on my shoulder I sucked her clit into my mouth and she gripped my head and shoulder immediately. I licked and slurped until she started moaning, then I slid one finger inside of her and moaned at how tight, hot, and wet she was.

Her knees buckled, so I used my free arm to hold her up. Her moaning grew louder. Her head flung back. Her pussy squeezed my finger tighter. Her grip on my shoulder tightened.

"I'm about to cum," she warned me.

I removed my mouth from her clit so I could see that shit. Her cum started sliding down my finger and I almost nutted just at the sight of hers.

"It's like that?" I mumbled in captivation while I continued to watch.

She fell into me and I lifted her and put her in the center of the bed. Jess put her feet on the bed and spread her legs. This was where it was supposed to end... but I couldn't stop. I pulled my boxers down slowly to give her time to stop me... she still didn't.

Her legs closed at the sight of what was between mine and I smiled as I crawled towards her. I wasn't this cocky for nothing. A nigga looked good and the dick was good too.

"You changing your mind?" I kissed her before she had a chance to answer.

Since she couldn't answer me with her mouth she wrapped her legs around me and pulled me closer to her.

I looked into her eyes and told her to, "Put me where you want me."

"Nah, you go where you wanna be."

"Why you always tryna run shit?"

Her giggle made me smile as she shrugged and grabbed my dick. She put me at her opening and looked back into my eyes. I slid into her gently and watched as her eyes closed and mouth opened.

"*I'm* running this shit," I reminded her as I fought the desire to close my own eyes.

I felt why that nigga wanted to lock her ass down. Slowly I pulled out and went back in long and deep. Prepared to dig up any desire she had for that nigga or anyone else besides me.

"You hear me, Jess?"

"Yes, Vega. You running this shit. You running this shit."

Jess looked at me briefly as I lifted myself slightly and pushed her right leg towards her arm pit. My strokes went even deeper. I gripped her waist and watched as her cum covered my dick just as it had done my finger.

"I swear I didn't mean to fall for you, girl. But I couldn't help myself. You made me."

She bit her lip and looked down at the connection of us. How she had my dick gleaming.

"Shut up, Vega."

"No. If we ending this shit we're ending it right. You're like... my best friend. A best friend that I can kiss and lay up with. And fuck and make love to."

"Please, Vega." Her face contorted. Her legs started trembling like she was about to cum, but she wrapped them around me tightly.

"What I'm gon' do when I can't kick it with you every day?" My strokes went deeper. Slower. "Who I'm gon' smoke with and lay up with?" Faster. Longer. "Who gon' accept my crazy ass like you?"

"Vega," she whispered. Her hands went to my stomach. Like she thought that would stop me. "I'm about to cum."

I felt that shit. Her walls gripped my dick tighter. She was feeling too fucking good.

"Jess, stop squeezing my dick like that. Just cum."

"I... can't... help... it... it... won't... let... go..." she grunted, raising her back off of the bed.

"Then cum and let go."

"I can't, Vega," she whined with a distressed look on her face.

She pulled me down to her and held me close. Still not letting me go.

"Cum, Jess," I begged.

The tight grip. The heat. The wetness. It was about to make me cum and I'll be damned if I nut before she do. She cried out and dropped her legs. I started stroking her quicker but that just made her grip me even tighter.

"Vegaaa, stop!"

"Not until you cum."

"I can't take it. I'm scared. You feel so good. What are you doing to me?"

I stopped and looked at her. Her eyes opened, full of tears, and she blinked until they dried up.

"Making sure you never forget me, but you gotta trust me, Jess. Let me in. Stop holding back."

Jess closed her eyes again and her head shook slowly. She stroked my cheeks a few times before pulling me down to her. We kissed deeply. More passionately than I'd ever kissed a woman before. I gripped the sheets above her head with one hand and her cheek with the other.

When I felt her body relax and her pussy release me I started stroking her again. Her lips trembled against mine. Her hands scratched my back before returning to my face. She gasped for air and lifted her back from the bed. I laid her back flat and continued to stroke her deep and slow.

"Vegaaa."

"Give it to me."

Finally, she let herself go and she came. I stayed in for as long as I could before pulling out and shooting my seeds in my hand. I sat on the edge of the bed with my head down and gave myself time to compose before standing and washing my hands.

I cut on the shower and turned to go and get her, but she was already walking inside. Jessica tried to walk past me to the shower without looking at me, but I grabbed her forearm and pulled her into me.

"Why you do that?" She asked avoiding my eyes.

I looked down at her and noticed that her eyebrows were wrinkled in anger.

"Do what?" I pulled her head up and made her look me in my eyes.

"Make me… make me…"

"Mine?"

She nodded and pulled her eyes away from me again.

"I get that our paths are leading us in two different directions, Jess, but when they do cross… I need to be sure that you know that this is real. And that that pussy will always belong to me. You wanna give another nigga your heart in the meantime that's cool, but we *will* meet again. And I want that pussy throbbing at the same rate of your heart every time we meet."

"But why, Vega? Why did you have to talk to me while you were inside of me? Kiss me like that. Touch me like that. Why did you have to make me cum? I literally didn't want to let you go. It felt like you became a part of me. Why would you tie your soul to mine like that?"

"Cause that's what matters most. I told you I wanted you. Now I'll always have you."

Her arms wrapped around my neck and she pulled me down to her for a kiss. If she wanted to fuck around with her ex that's cool. If she wanna fuck around with other niggas in the meantime of us that's cool. But no matter who she called herself being with, when Vega Freeman resurfaced, all of her belonged to me.

Grace

I wasn't as excited about the prom as B and Jessie were. I still hadn't reached out to my parents and they hadn't put forth any effort to contact me. If it was that easy for Andy to find me I'm sure it could have been just as easy for them too.

But they didn't care.

And that didn't surprise me.

Braille's family planned on gathering at her home to see her and Lorenzo off and I didn't want to feel like I was intruding so I went to Hanif's house to get dressed. He and I were doing *so* good. There were still times when he got on my damn nerves, but for the most part he was opening up and letting me in.

When I was done getting dressed I walked into his den and was faced with the surprise of my life. Hanif wasn't in there alone. Braille, Lorenzo, Ms. Josephine, Mr. Edward, Jessica, Vega, Coach Power, Elle, Rule, and Camryn were all in there with him. Waiting for me.

I cried so hard Jessie had to redo my makeup. When she was done they all left and Hanif and I were alone. Man, I was so in my feelings I didn't even want to go to the prom. No one had ever put something so thoughtful together for me.

My first thought was that it was B or Jessie's idea… so when he told me that it was his I fell for him even more. I asked him why and his simple reply was that he wanted me to know that I wasn't alone.

I wasn't alone.

We stayed at the prom for about thirty minutes before I was ready to go. Braille and Lorenzo had already left and as relaxed as Jessica looked on Vega's chest I figured they would be leaving soon too. Instead of going right back to Hanif's place I asked him to take me home. My home. Well… my old home. To see my parents.

If they still had their same routines my father would have been in the middle of the couch watching Cops and drinking a beer while my mother was in the kitchen at the table flipping through magazines that were years old.

What a life.

"You sure you wanna do this?" Hanif asked as he cut his car off.

I nodded and inhaled deeply. He came and let me out and we walked to my front door hand in hand. I started to use my key, but I removed it from my key chain and knocked instead. Hanif massaged my shoulders until the door opened.

When I thought of this moment I wasn't sure how I'd feel seeing my father... but now that I did... I didn't feel anything. My father's face went from relief to anger. His hand raised to come down on my face and I waited for the hit for some reason... but I never felt it. I opened my eyes and saw Hanif's hand wrapped around my father's wrist.

Tears immediately filled my eyes as he walked into their home and pushed my father back in the process.

"That's what you not gon' do, sir. You got a problem with her you take it up with me." Hanif released his wrist and my father took a step back.

"And who the hell are you?"

My eyes closed again.

"I'm her boyfriend."

They opened quickly. *My boyfriend? Since when? Did he mean that?*

"No... Andy is her boyfriend."

"Was. He's out of the picture now. I'm here."

"Why are you here?" My father asked me.

I tried to hand him the key as my mother walked into the hallway.

"Baby!" She yelled running towards me.

"Trina..." My father's voice stopped her immediately.

I smiled and lowered my head to avoid crying.

"It's fine, Ma," I whispered.

She walked over to him and stood by his side. Her head lowered and I realized where I'd gotten that from. Her. Hanif saw it too. He walked over to me and grabbed the key. I thought he was going to give it to my father, but he handed it to my mother. She looked at him briefly before lowering her head again.

Hanif's mouth twisted in disgust as he shook his head.

"That's your daughter," he mumbled in disbelief.

"Let's just go, Neef."

I walked out and he followed behind me. With each step I took I felt lighter and heavier at the same time. The realization that I'd never heard either of my parents tell me that they loved me hit me hard. But at that moment... I no longer gave a fuck. I refused to turn into my mother. I refused to settle. I refused to be weak.

I opened the door of the car but Hanif closed it, grabbed me, and pulled me into his arms.

"I'm so sorry you had to grow up with them." His voice was low and tender as he spoke into my hair. "Fuck what I've said in the past. Never hide your feelings from me. Never. Never hide from me like that, Grace. However you feel you show that shit and tell me. Don't bow down like your mother does. Ever. To no fucking body."

No longer able to hold my tears in they escaped my eyes and I cried on him just as hard as I did the first time we met.

"It's okay, baby. I got you. I swear I do. I got you, Grace."

I held him tighter. Closer. My body shook harder. His hand stroked my hair as he held me with his other arm.

And then... I felt the softest breeze of air. If I could imagine how the Holy Spirit felt that would be it. In the heat of the humid night air the breeze sent chills down my spine. I pulled myself out of Hanif's chest and looked into his eyes.

"Did you feel that?" I asked.

"Feel what?"

"Nothing. Can we go home?"

"Whatever you want."

He opened the door and I got in with a calm and peace I'd never felt before. I looked at their house one last time as Hanif's hand enveloped mine. Perfectly content with the fact that this would be my last time visiting. My last time crying over my fucked up childhood. My last time giving them power over my emotions. My last time seeking the love and acceptance outside of myself that must be found within. My last time.

Hanif

My plan was to head straight to the beach house I rented for us in Biloxi, but I was so caught up in how good Grace looked that I forgot both of our bags at the house. Her hair was up in a slick bun for the first time since I'd known her.

Her eyeshadow was smoky and her lipstick was black. It gave her an edgy more mature look and I loved it! Her dress was black, sheer, and lace. The front was super short. Mid-thigh. But the back came down to the floor. The sleeves were off of her shoulders and they stopped at her elbows. The front of the dress had a low v neck cut that showed me enough to make my dick hard but hid enough to have me wanting to take her home so I could see more.

The shit with her parents threw me off. I wasn't expecting her to want to go over there, and she didn't even get to have her talk and closure. It didn't matter, though. I'd made myself the protector of not just her body, but her heart as well, so she was gon' be well taken care of.

On the ride back to my house we both were quiet. I held her hand and caressed her fingers every once in a while. She'd looked over at me and smile. When we pulled up to my house and I saw Pria's car in the driveway I groaned. I broke up with her the day Grace came up to my shop acting a damn fool.

I hadn't heard from her since then, and couldn't give her any of my attention or focus now. Grace was my *only* concern. I cut the car off and she looked over at me with puffy eyes.

"Why is she here, Neef? I thought you said you broke up with her?"

Her voice was low and tired. No attitude or anger. Just a desperate need for clarification. I cut on the lights in the car to make sure she could see me.

"I did. I don't know why she's here, but I'm going to get rid of her."

To reassure her I pulled her face to mine and kissed her. Her hand went to my face but I pulled it down to give Pria a good look. Grace pulled away from me and smiled.

"You're mean. Why you do that in front of that girl?"

I smiled and kissed her forehead.

"Ain't shit changed," I mumbled as I got out of my car.

"Really, Hanif?" Pria asked as I unlocked the door.

"What's up, Pria? I'm kind of in a rush."

I put one leg in the house, grabbed our bags from behind the door, and locked it behind me. If she thought she was coming inside she was sadly mistaken.

"Where you going?"

"What do you need?"

"You. I... miss us."

"I'm sorry, Pria, but it's over. I've moved on. You need to too."

"I put up with a lot of shit to be with you, Hanif. You've cheated on me multiple times. Put me out of your spot in the middle of the night after sex. Disappeared for days without saying a word to me. Now you want to just end it for her?"

"You should be glad she's taking me off of your hands. From the sound of it I ain't no good. Not to you anyway."

I tried to walk away but she grabbed my arm.

"Just... tell me why. Why her? Why is she pulling you away from me when nobody else could?"

I turned slightly and looked towards my car.

"None of the other women mattered to me. They were just a fuck. But Grace... she's different. She needs me and I need her. I want to love her and be with her. I've never wanted to love anyone else."

"Not even me?"

My eyes returned to Pria.

"Not even you." She released me and nodded. "I'm sorry."

"No it's... I asked."

"Is that it? I really need to get back to my baby."

She chuckled and took a step back.

"Yea. Sure. That's it."

"Okay... well..."

I pointed towards her car hoping she'd get the point. Her feet dragged slowly to her car. I waited outside until she was on her way down the street. Then I put our bags in the backseat and got inside.

"What was that about, Hanif?"

"Nothing of importance."

She didn't question me. She didn't crinkle her nose like she did when I said some shit she didn't like. She put her head on the headrest and closed her eyes peacefully. Like she trusted me.

"Grace?"

"Neef?"

I smiled as she looked at me.

"I love you."

Her eyes closed and her chest rose from the deep breath she took.

"You do?"

"I do."

Grace opened her eyes as a tear fell from the right one. Her and these happy tears. I'd always been infatuated with her innocent eyes… but now… they had darkened in desire. I couldn't stop staring into those eyes. She snatched my heart and soul with those eyes.

"You're the first person to ever tell me that, Hanif. Besides Andy, and he didn't mean it."

"You mean… besides your parents?"

"No. Period."

I looked away from her as my eyes watered. *No one? No one had ever told this beautiful creature that she was loved?* All logic left me. For the first time in my life I allowed myself to be led by my emotions fully. I got out of the car and made my way over to her side.

"Neef… what are you…"

When I had her seatbelt unbuckled I turned her sideways and pulled her panties down. She unbuttoned and unzipped my pants at the same speed. I pulled her ass to the edge of the seat, gripped her waist, and looked into her eyes.

As I entered her I told her again.

"I love you, Grace."

I couldn't even get all of me inside of her. Her legs wrapped around me as she leaned back and across the center console.

"I love you," I muttered as I pulled myself out of her and dove in again.

"Hanif," she whispered breathlessly. "I love you too."

She spread her legs wider and was able to take more of me in.

"Fuck," I muttered as she grabbed my wrists. "I love you. I love you. I love you."

How many times would it take to make up for years of not hearing this?

"Neef, I need you closer."

I leaned down and allowed her to wrap her arms and legs around me. Fucked myself up because I felt her nectar splattering onto my stomach. Her legs trembled and fell and she moaned into my ear as she came. Finally, I could slide all of me inside. And go so deep it felt as if I connected her heart to mine.

When her orgasm released her she commanded me to, "Say it again," into my neck before licking it.

"I love you."

I felt her laugh softly as she wrapped her legs back around me.

"I love you too. I've loved you since I laid eyes on you, Hanif. I love you."

Why did she have to say that shit?

"I don't want to stop. You're not on any birth control, are you?"

"No. Please, don't stop."

"You need to get on some."

"Okay."

"Soon, Grace."

"Okaaay."

I bit down on her cheek and filled her with a few more strokes before I pulled out and let my seeds hit the concrete.

Her arms and legs wrapped back around me and she held me tighter than she ever had. I hugged her back until I gathered my strength and tried to let her go but she wouldn't let me.

"Baby, let me go so we can go."

"No. Ion want to."

I smiled and tried to remove her arms but she held me tighter.

"Grace… we can cuddle when we get to the beach house."

"Neef!"

"Fine."

I picked her up and sat in the passenger's seat of my car. With her arms and legs wrapped around me. Stroking her back until she drifted off to sleep. When I heard her quiet mumbling I shook my head and pulled myself out of her. I let the seat back some and laid her down hoping she wouldn't wake up. She didn't.

Quietly, I shut her door and made my way behind the wheel. As soon as I cut the car on I cut the radio off and looked over at her. She was knocked out. I ran my finger down her nose gently and kissed it before reversing and heading to Biloxi.

Braille

I woke up this morning sick to my stomach. Not the normal sick... but a sick that signaled something was wrong. My heart was heavy. Racing. My head was throbbing. I was shaking. I called Zo, but he didn't answer. I checked out my parents and they were good.

Jessie and Grace were good.

I called Cam and Rule and neither of them answered their phones.

I called Lorenzo again. He didn't answer again.

I called Jessie back and had her to call Vega on three-way, but he didn't answer.

I called Lorenzo again. He didn't answer again.

Why wasn't he answering?

Why wasn't he answering?

God, why wasn't he answering?

Finally, Cam called me back and told me to come and let her and Rule in the house. I did... and the looks on their faces scared the shit out of me.

"What's going on?" I asked looking from one to the other.

"Have you eaten anything? Let's go sit in the kitchen," Rule said softly.

"No. I'm not hungry. What's going on?"

"Braille..." Camryn started but I held my hand up and stopped her as tears flooded and fell from my eyes.

"No, Camryn. Just... tell me. Tell me what you need to tell me."

She looked at Rule and so did I.

"Um..." He cleared his throat and ran his hand down his neck. "Yesterday, two of Lorenzo's corner boys were arrested."

"What? Why didn't he tell me?"

"He didn't want you to worry. This morning he held an emergency meeting with his camp." Rule paused and I clutched my heart. "Everyone at the meeting was arrested, B. Including Lorenzo."

I closed my eyes and shook my head.

"No... that's... I just left him like two hours ago, Rule. I was just with him."

"I know, baby, but as soon as he dropped you off at home he went to his meeting. He was arrested. Vega was pulling up when they were bringing everyone out of the warehouse. He saw Zo, but Zo motioned for him to leave. Vega is at my place now. We're going to do all that we can…"

He was still talking. His lips were still moving. But nothing that he was saying was registering in my brain. I felt my knees give out on me but there was nothing I could do to stop them. Rule grabbed me and pulled me into his chest.

"Why? Why didn't he just stop? I told him to stop. I told him to stop."

"I'm sorry, B. I'm going to do all that I can," Rule assured me as Camryn turned her back to me.

I saw her shoulders shaking and that made me cry even more because this was real. He was really gone.

"He can't go to jail, Rule! I can't do this shit without him! I love him!" I sobbed.

"I know, baby. I know. But we all knew that this was a possibility because of his lifestyle."

"Oh yea? Well did we all know that I would end up pregnant?"

"What?!" Rule and Camryn asked in unison.

TO BE CONTINUED...

CPSIA information can be obtained
at www.ICGtesting.com
Printed in the USA
LVHW02s2340070818
586327LV00009B/323/P

9 781544 611532